Paro Anand has been honoured with the Sahitya Akademi Bal Sahitya Puraskar Award, 2017 for her book *Wild Child*, now published as *Like Smoke* with additional content. Her book, *No Guns at My Son's Funeral* was on the IBBY Honor List and has been translated into German and Spanish. *The Little Bird Who Held the Sky up with His Feet* was on 1001 Books to Read Before You Grow Up, an international gold standard of the world's best children's literature. BBC Hindi selected her on their #100Women Project, a project highlighting the challenges and achievements of women in India.

the other

Stories of Difference

PARO ANAND

SPEAKING
TIGER

Published by Speaking Tiger Publishing Pvt. Ltd
4381/4, Ansari Road, Daryaganj
New Delhi 110002

First published in paperback by Speaking Tiger in 2018

Copyright © Paro Anand 2018

ISBN: 978-93-88070-33-1
eISBN: 978-93-88070-12-6

10 9 8 7 6 5 4 3 2 1

Typeset in Garamond Premier Pro by SÜRYA, New Delhi
Printed at Sanat Printers, Kundli

To
Keshav
Aditi and Susan
Uday and Parth
Gia and Nadia
You light up my life
And give me the confidence to explore the dark side

Leaving behind nights of terror and fear
I rise
Into a daybreak that's wondrously clear
I rise

—Maya Angelou

contents

she walks between raindrops

She was way, way out of my league. Like way. I knew, of course, I could never even aspire to be with her. Not in the way I wanted to be with her. I mean, look at her. Just look at her.

It was like there was music in her step, like she was walking to a tune. Music in everything she did. Her words came out to a tune, she floated instead of walking. And if it rained, then she would walk out into the rain. And I kid you not, she would be walking between raindrops. Like the rain wouldn't fall on her. Except a few drops that would kiss her cheeks.

Umm, okay, I agree, that is a bit cheesy. I just thought of it because once, it was drizzling and everyone was coming into school all damp and plastered hair. I was watching her, wishing I could rush out and hold an umbrella for her (which I could not), but she came in, all fresh, bouncy hair and a couple of raindrops on her cheeks and shoulder. She was laughing and smiling and the sun came out. It really was as if she had walked between raindrops. Yes, she...she was perfect. And perfectly out of my league. As I've already said. And I say it every day. Because I need to remind myself, because my heart won't get the message and won't settle anywhere else. On anyone else. Not that, to be honest, there was anyone else who was an option for me. I was option-less. Like zilch.

If she was way above my league, then I was way below anyone else's. I was on no one's wish list. And I am not being a poor martyred boy, it's quite simply the truth.

If I were to look at myself in the mirror...and when I say 'if', I mean it literally. Because I don't. Look in mirrors or into any reflective surfaces. In fact, the opposite. I am super careful not to look at shop windows or into a car because then I can see myself. I have matt finish on the photographs in my room and in fact, have insisted on the same through the house. So that I don't catch a glimpse of myself by accident.

No, I am not paranoid, just...weird. Just, okay, let's say, odd. Look, I know there are a lot of my classmates who are totally acceptable looking. To the extent that they are even good looking, but they are constantly fussing and complaining that they are ugly. I mean please.

Have you seen me? And they have the gall to say in my presence, *my* presence that they think that *they* are ugly? I mean how insensitive can they be?

All right, I may as well come out and say it. I am Special. Yes, everyone's special—each unique in their own ways, but mine comes with a capital S. As in what used to be called handicapped or even deformed in the bad old days before political correctness became a thing. I am glad no one is allowed to tell me I am deformed, but I can hear the capital in Special and I know that it's one and the same thing. The change of a word doesn't change a fact.

And the fact is that I am very thin, very fragile, wear thick glasses. But here's the kicker. I carry a urine bag around. Like outside my body. Yes, of course it's camouflaged with a cloth bag that hides the tubes and everything. But everyone knows what's in the lumpy lump hanging on my side. And it is totally gross. It grosses *me* out, so, of course it grosses others out even more.

Not that anyone is mean about it. Or talks about it, or even mentions it. But if someone trips or pushes past me and the bag kind of squishes, I see the squirms. There was one guy when I first joined school who would try and push others on to me, on to the bag. It was mortifying. My schoolmates would try and be polite, but obviously they had these horrified looks on their faces that said, 'Oh no, did I touch the thing?'

That was when I fell in love. Deeply and madly. And forever. Because she came up and yelled at the pathetic bully to stay away from me, to quit his stupid pranks and if she ever, ever caught him doing that or anything else to me, she would punch him so hard that he'd need to be taken away in a body bag. Or something like that. I was standing helplessly to one side. Helpless because I couldn't fight my own battles and helpless because I knew I was in love. But mostly helpless because I knew how futile it was going to be. I mean who falls in love with a guy who carries around a bag of pee, right? Of course right.

The best thing about her was that she didn't treat me special. After that one time when she stuck up for me, she'd always just say hi, and give me a light smack between my shoulders and call me 'dude' although there really was nothing dude-ish about me. She'd ask me about what I thought about a movie or did I find a Math test too hard, like she had.

See, the others were all pretty kind. But like, too kind. You know, in a 'be kind to dumb animals' kind sort of way. They were too cautious, too overly solicitous. It made it more uncomfortable than if they'd just been mean. No, that's probably not right. I am sure I would have hated that. But, honestly, I could see the pity in their eyes. That they were wary of me. Basically, they didn't know what to do with me. Even if they wanted to, they didn't know how to be friends with someone like me.

But that was not the same with Sanjana. No, she was just friends with me, the way she was friends with everyone else in the class. That was why I thought that she was the coolest. And that is why I thought she walked between raindrops. As far as

I was concerned, no one and nothing could touch her. Sadly, that included me. Though sometimes, most times, when she was standing right there, I really, really wanted to reach out and touch her hand, her arm. But I didn't. I did not want her to get all weird on me. I didn't think she had any clue about how I felt about her.

See, it's not like I have any redeeming features. Like, when you read about someone like me in a story, the guy (or girl) will be a genius in a broken body. I mean, look at Stephen Hawking, his body was like a total mess. (I am not being nasty, just stating the truth), but his mind...well, we all know that he was a totally cool genius. Genius for his Theory of Time and cool because he said, 'Life would be tragic if it weren't funny' which is the mantra I live by. And by the way, he was totally the very coolest because he appeared on *The Big Bang Theory* which is my favourite show as it's full of nerds like me. Oh and by the way, did you know that he teamed up with his daughter, Lucy, and wrote some awesome children's books about outer space?

Anyway, this isn't a story about Mr Hawking, but about me. So yeah, although his body was a total mess, like mine, his mind was super brilliant.

Which mine is not. Far from it. I wish I could have either had a very clever mind, or some mental issues as well. I know it's a weird thing to wish for, but, think about it. It is super, super hard to have a broken body and an average mind. It leaves you stranded in the middle of nowhere-land. If I was attention deficient or dyslexic or something, then, wow, I would have something solid to put the blame on.

And my parents' and teachers' expectations would have been titrated down to a manageable level. As it is, however, I see in everyone's eyes that they are saying, 'Look, you need to be brilliant in your mind, because you have to make up for your body.' I know that. Oh, don't I know that? But I can't make my mind stick to one thing at a time. It's like there's a grasshopper piloting my brain. And just when it settles on one thing, it leaps off into the opposite direction. Maybe I have attention deficit disorder, you know, ADD. But just not enough to make me certifiably even more special. Besides, if it were so, I may have been put into a school for multiply disabled kids. In which case, I would never have met her. Sanjana.

Her. I look at her now and wow. She is looking straight right back at me. As though she can hear my thoughts. I wasn't talking out loud, was I? I look around, did everyone else hear me too? Yep. I am afraid so. They are all staring at me like I am an alien. I probably am. In this world of beautiful faces and bladders inside bodies, I am an alien.

Turns out, I hadn't been talking out loud. Thank goodness. Sanjana was made one of the three team captains. And she got to pick the first member of her team. And she called my name. MY name. I mean, you probably know that my name is not the one that gets called out first. Of course not. And I totally understand that. That's why my grasshopper mind was nowhere near to paying attention. As always, I thought it was a long, long way before my name got called to join a team. Me and another couple of the usual kids got left to the last usually. The dregs of society. Oh I am not being bitter or anything. I get it. If the game or competition or whatever asks for physical prowess, then me and fat girl over there and runny-nosed Allergy Anks were not going to be called. If the game required mental agility, then me and Wheezy Whoosh and Slow Slowena were the last picks. And when we were the last ones left in the mix, you could see the teams sizing us up and wondering which one of us dregs was going to be the lesser of the burden, the least liability. I'm just facing facts. And when we did get picked, we walked up to a team of fallen faces and uncomfortable silence as they moved aside reluctantly to let us in. Moved aside even more for me, everyone making sure that they were avoiding my pee bag.

So you can imagine my enormous surprise when she called my name first. Everyone else was surprised too. I was pleased, of course, but also mortified. She'd put her faith in me and I was only going to let her down. There was nothing else I could possibly do.

We were to do this play, see, and it was supposed to be a funny take on any fairy or folk tale but with a modern twist. Like in old stories there were a lot of things that are politically so very incorrect in today's climate. So we had to make it overly politically correct and funny, but at the same time, sensitive to the situation. I know it sounds corny. But I can't explain it any better. As I have already said, I wasn't totally paying attention.

I whispered to Sanjana (which was so cool, by the way, I'd never been that close to her—and she smelled so awesome—of honey and butterflies, or something romantic like that. Not that I've smelt butterflies, but you know what I mean.) 'You didn't have to do that, you know?' Of course she knew what I'd meant, but she still asked the inevitable 'Do what?'

'You didn't have to pick me, not first anyway. There are so many better candidates...' She took my hand, slyly, as though we were actually boyfriend and girlfriend holding hands in school without the teacher seeing. Oh my god, my heart almost burst out of my chest. I bet everyone could see it beating a mad march, my chest was so bony. 'I wanted you,' she whispered back.

Wanted me? Like, Sanjana, the beautiful, the walking-between-raindrops Sanjana wanted me, like truly? Really? I couldn't believe my luck. Had she just chosen me for like, more than just the play? Did she like, *want* me, want me? The way I wanted her to want me?

I spent the rest of the lesson in a daze. Apparently, our play went really really well. And even more oddly, I was very good as the dorky prince who chooses a poor, beautiful Cinderella in a world where beauty is looked down upon. But I choose her for her confidence and strength and not because she is a beauty. Sadly, Sanjana didn't act that part, so I didn't get to dance with her. I danced with Elena who was a good sport about dancing with me, pee bag and all.

But something shifted after that, it was like a veil had been lifted and people could see me behind the pee bag. Like as a whole person. I don't know exactly what changed. But something had. Sometimes, I guess, it just takes a moment. One person to treat you like a normal person. And others start to think of you like a normal person too.

I am not saying that there was an 'ahhhhh' moment and I went from being pee-bag boy to person, but just the fact that Sanjana had picked me and I had done all right, made others think that way. And that's when it hit me. It wasn't the others, or at least, it wasn't only the others. It was me too. It was in that one moment of being picked first that I realized that I was more than a pee bag. It made me feel okay about being me, bag and all. And maybe that is what made the difference too.

Okay, now this isn't one of those great fairy tales where Sanjana and I go off hand in hand into the sunset. No, it isn't. It did break my heart more than a little bit when she started going out with someone else. And no, I didn't find the love of my life in anyone else either. But at least I felt included, or a little less excluded at any rate. And I got a little confidence that somewhere out there, there could be a girl for me in my life. Could be a fellow pee-bagger, or not. But whatever, at least I had a little spark of hope in me.

Sometimes a fairy tale can have a happy ending without the sunset and roses, I guess. At least, mine did. And I will love the girl who walked between raindrops forever after.

best friends forever

'How's my peanut?'

'Did my puchka have a good day?'

'I never expect anything else but the best from you, strawberry.'

Dad always called me by food items. Especially when he was really happy with me. Which, I have to say, was most of the time. Mum, on the other hand, was the more practical one. And yes, you can hear the sneer when I say 'practical'. I mean, I love her and all, she's my mum, after all. But she always called me Saudamini. In this very formal way, almost. No pet names and cute goofy loving terms. This, even when I told her I hated my name. I mean, who, in this day and age thinks of naming their child after a grandmother? Realllly? There were so many better names out there. Saudamini may have been a great name back then, but now...? Luckily, though, she was one of the few people who called me by my full name. Dad, as I've said, called me by food items.

Dad was really cool, most of the time. He was one of the happiest people I knew. Like, if Mum was annoyed with him, and even if she was being unreasonable (much of the time, I have to say), he'd just apologize and put his arms around her and hold her till the anger went out. Sort of how you throw a blanket over a fire and smother it to cool it. He did it with me too. If Mum and I were in a flaming row, he'd put his arms around us, one at a time, or he'd try and get us both into his wingspan at once, but it didn't work. Not every time at any rate.

Between Mum and me, without his realizing it, there'd be a simmering resentment left over and that could explode any moment. Mostly, we tried to have our fights when he was away. So that we could fight it out properly and not be smothered into what he hoped was loving silence. But that didn't happen so often. They both worked together in a company that they'd started when they were still at college. So they went off to work together and came back together. And since they'd grown up together, they had all the same friends, so it wasn't as though they'd have a night out with their individual friends.

Although they were childhood friends, they still had their disagreements and as time went by and I hit the teen years, those disagreements turned their gaze more and more on me.

Dad was more the YES parent. He more or else less always said 'yes' when I asked him anything. Whether it was a school trip, a pair of high heels, a sleepover with friends, whatever. He'd say yes. And that, of course, left Mum to be the NO parent. She'd say no and I'd be left in the middle, hoping Dad would dig his heels in and make her agree with him—with us. But that didn't happen too often. Sometimes, I'd have to prime him for the task. I'd tell him in advance what I was going to ask and I'd make him promise that he was going to stand up for me and not back down to her unreasonableness. But more often than not, when the moment came and she brought her gritted teeth and flashing eyes out, he'd have her in a hug and shrug his shoulders helplessly at me. Sometimes I wished he was more of a man.

I mean, true, why should men be mean, why should they have the ultimate veto? But that's the way most of my friends' homes were. The Dad wore the pants and wielded the veto vote. That's just how it was. But somehow, I ended up with a Dad who was softer and a Mum who was tougher, the one who wore the pants in our home. Not that Dad wore the skirts or saris. Pff, that would be weird.

Sometimes I actually felt a bit sorry for Mum. Not often, but sometimes, she'd look to Dad to be the No and he'd see the look, but turn a blind eye. He was good at that. So I felt for her sometimes. Though, as I've said, not often.

So anyway, it was Mum who first started kicking up a fuss about Aarav coming over. Well, not about his coming over, really, but more that she didn't want us together in my room with the door shut. 'Come over in a group, or sit in the living room,' she'd insist. And my, 'that's so lame,' went down as well as one could expect it to. About as well as the, 'well I insist,' from her did.

Aarav was okay with it, though he did try once with a, 'we're just friends,' line. But she was having none of it, so he and I sat feeling foolish in our very formal living room, sipping iced tea (of all things, as though we were a hundred and one). We talked awkwardly for about twenty minutes, with Mum pretending she had something very important to do which brought her out through the living room every two minutes, (literally, she came in ten times in those twenty minutes). Finally, Aarav said, 'Um, I guess I should go now,' and I said, 'Okay,' almost before the words had left his mouth.

On Mum's eleventh trip through, she feigned surprise and disappointment with a very lame, 'Ohhhh, has he gone already?'

We were bitterly bickering about it when Dad walked in. He'd taken our dog out for a run for about an hour or more.

'Heyyyyy,' he said as soon as he saw us. He didn't need to even hear our fight. Our body language was so battleground. 'What are my two favourite girls talking about? Come here, peanut.' He was already approaching us with his arms stretched out, but he was too sweaty for the hug thing. And frankly, I was just too mad.

Mum turned on him and practically snarled, 'She thinks she's so grown up that she can take boys up to her bedroom and do who knows what behind locked doors...'

'MUM!' I shouted as loudly and fiercely as I could, 'First of all, it's not boys—it's one—my best friend. And secondly, I don't know what you were up to at my age, but all the whatnot I wanted to get up to was talk to my best friend. TALK—just TALK!' I added a 'you sicko' under my breath.

'Then why did you need to lock the door?'

'It wasn't locked, how many times do I have to tell you?'

She gave me her long-suffering sigh and said, 'Fine, then why did you need to *shut* the door?' She turned triumphantly to poor, sweaty Dad so I turned to him too, appealing.

'Because you are in and out of the room like a hundred and twenty times. Like even when we were in the stupid living room, you were hovering like a...like a...' (oh I wanted to say witch or something worse, but I didn't).

'Dad, it's impossible for me to have a proper conversation with anyone if she's around. She won't let me have any privacy. It was soooooo embarrassing.'

There was a moment of silence. We were waiting for Dad's verdict. He slid me a look that

I understood immediately. He was telling me that he actually agreed with me but was going to take Mum's side a little, just to soften her up. And also, if he didn't, she'd bite his head right off. Just like a black widow spider.

'So we have no problem with his coming over. It's just that we need you to be careful...' Dad's voice trailed off weakly. Any fool could tell that he wasn't really convinced with his own argument. And Mum was one such. Fool, I mean. She shot him a dirty look, took a deep breath which meant that she was thinking, 'Oh lord, I've got to handle this on my own, he's so useless when it comes to being sensible and strict.'

And there, of course, came the lecture for the nth time about how I was not a child anymore and there were certain boundaries that had to be maintained between boys and girls now and that raging hormones in teens....blah blah blah!

'Look, I don't know if you've ever even *heard* of a platonic relationship with someone from the opposite *sex*...' Yep, I did emphasize the word as much as I could and got a most satisfactory wince from Mum in return. So I continued, 'But privacy to do *what?*'

I turned to Dad then and appealed to him. But he was already headed towards her with his arms outstretched so she got distracted and shouted at him to stay away. He was sweaty and full of dog hair. They laughed as he chased her. And I really felt that if anyone needed chaperoning it would be them.

I left, really annoyed. This would be a good time to call Aarav. I could chat away, without her hovering.

'I'm really sorry, dude, my mum's just the worst.'

'It's cool, I guess they just don't get that we are really just good friends and it's irrelevant that you're a girl and I, well, I...well, I'm...me.'

And that was enough talk on Mum. We went on to talk about all the other stuff that we'd been wanting to talk about when she was in and out of the room. Nothing earth-shattering, just stuff. That was the best thing about Aarav, we could talk about all kinds of things. Like, he'd even help me decide what to wear to a party. And I never, ever went clothes shopping without him. He had the best taste in clothes. That's the kind of best friend he was.

Anyway, when I came back down, Dad had worked something like a miracle. He'd hugged a compromise out of Mum that Aarav and I could be in my room, only, we shouldn't shut the door. I had to hug him then, sweat and all. I don't care about not shutting the door. I mean, Aarav and I literally just talk. Unless I'm trying out some new outfit for a party and trying to decide which one I look least hideous in. And even then, I come out of the bathroom and show him. I'm not changing in front of him or anything. I mean, yu-ck.

Anyway, it's nice to be able to chat to him on our own instead of in-the-stupid-living-room thing. Now there is a hot new topic to talk about. I discuss all my crushes with Aarav. And his advice is always great. He doesn't talk much about his love interests. There haven't been many. Or any. Actually. Anyway...

This new boy had just arrived in our class. He was really cute. He's from some other country, some exotic mixed parentage and all of us were dying and vying to get to know more and be his friends. Of course, there were others who got there first, so Aarav and I just had the fleeting pleasure of a nod and a hi, how are you kind of moment.

Later, in my room (finalllly), I confessed to Aarav that I'd fallen in love—also finallllly. This new kid—Daniel—made my heart beat faster, which, in turn, unfortunately made my palms a bit sweaty. 'I think I'm in love, bro. It's not the usual crush this time. I'm sure.'

There was a pause. And it went on a bit and for a terrible long moment, I suddenly had a panic attack wondering if Aarav was in love with me. I mean, he looked so sad. He looked as though the weight of it had suddenly fallen on his shoulders.

'What?' I said, unable to bear the silent tension anymore.

'*Nothing...*'

His voice was small and he'd somehow shrunk. Oh god, he was going to say it. And I loved him. A lot. But I didn't *love* him, love him, you know? What was I going to do? I certainly didn't want to lose my best friend.

'You know you can tell me, Aarav, what is it?' I tried to sound reassuring although I was the one who needed the reassurance myself.

'There, well, there's is something I've been needing to talk to you about.'

'Ok...ayyy,' I braced myself. Here it comes. Though inside my head I was saying, 'Shut up, shut up, don't say it. Don't say anything.'

'I...oh man, there's no easy way to say this. Wait, I...oh ma...an.'

He got up, he paced the floor. He turned to me, opened his mouth like, here it comes. But instead, he dropped his shoulders, shook his head, but he wouldn't look at me.

'No, you know, it's nothing, I can't.' But he was near tears now. And honestly, I was kind of relieved that he was backing off. I really didn't want to hear it. Like, if he told me he was in love with me, then... well then, it was going to ruin every single thing in the world. I mean, he couldn't be my best friend any longer. Not once he'd told me he loved me and I didn't love him back.

'Okay, look, don't worry about it. You don't have to tell me if you don't want to.'

He looked at me and I saw the tears leaking out of his eyes. His nose was starting to run, as though the tears were trying to find an alternate route. 'But I need to tell you, I can't lie anymore...' his voice was tiny, like a whisper. But a very broken one.

I had to be sensible about this. Even though I'm usually not good at doing practical. That's what was needed now. Bring on the sensible. Bring on the practical.

I didn't know what exactly I was going to say once he told me, but I could not be a friend and then not let him tell me what was weighing him down so much. What kind of friend would that be? He was always such a good listener to my woes. I guess it was my turn now.

'Look, come on, come, sit with me,' I patted the bed for him to come sit. Yeah, he nodded slowly, mouthing the word. He sat on my bed and I got up to shut the door, knowing that Mum was going to come home in a bit and then throw a hissy fit about broken promises, but this was a closed-door talk. I knew that much.

His head was slung so low that his chin was totally resting on his chest. His shoulders were slumped. He looked so small and sad that I knew I was going to really have to help him say it. I stroked his back. His shoulders were so tense.

I leaned my head on his shoulder, kissing the corner of it before laying my head there. He would be more comfortable if I was not looking at him.

'Say it, apple pie,' (getting to be more like my dad everyday) I whispered.

'I'm a girl...' he whispered back.

'What?!' I laughed, shoving him with my head. And he actually fell off the bed. I was giggling. 'What d'you mean you're such a girl? You mean that you don't have courage? You mean boys have more courage than girls?' And I was about to launch into this whole woman power spiel, but he held his finger up to shut me up, still looking down at his bare toes.

'No, I didn't say I'm "such a girl", I said, "I am a girl".'

He looked up at me straight in the eye and repeated it.

'I am a girl.'

No, you're not bubbled up inside my throat. I was standing now, though I didn't remember doing that. I thought I had my head on his shoulder. He was still sitting on the floor where he'd fallen when I shoved him.

'Ummm, dude, you don't know what you're talking about. Did you hit your head on something on your way here?'

'Sit down.' Command. He was commanding me to sit on my own bed. I sat. He'd never commanded me before.

'Look, I've been wanting—needing you to know this in a while. I...I...may be a boy by birth. But inside, like who I really am is not a boy, but a girl.'

'No,' was all that came out. I mean, I knew him

so well, knew everything about him. How was it remotely possible that I wouldn't know this? Besides, and most important, it just wasn't true. I knew it. Somehow, though, he didn't. So 'NO' was all I could say to him.

*

Later, much much later, I'm sitting in the living room. My head is on my dad's lap, Mum is stroking my shoulders. And I'm crying my heart out. I haven't even been able to tell them what it's about. But my heart's breaking. It's horrible. Just horrible.

'Something to do with Aarav?' Dad asks.

I nod yes.

'I knew it,' Mum is up and pacing immediately. 'I just *knew* it!' without even looking up, I can feel her turn ferociously onto Dad. Like all of this is his fault.

'I knew it was getting too much. All this best friend stuff is just...just...rubbish.'

'It's not like that, Mum,' I try and butt in. But she's not listening to me anymore. I can tell that her imagination has run wild and she's got a horror movie running through her head. And I realize right then that I can't tell them. I don't know how to tell them. And I don't know if they'll understand. Because I don't know how to process what I've just been told. I don't know if I can find the words. Ever.

I feel like I'm on my own. And I've just made it worse for myself by telling them this half truth that something was up between Aarav and me. I cannot, just cannot tell them that my best friend thinks he's a girl. I can't bear to think it myself. But what should I tell them instead? I can't have them thinking that he came on to me. He didn't. He would never. Now I almost wish he had.

And then it strikes me like a ton of bricks. I always thought, somewhere at the back of my stupid brain that Aarav was secretly in love with me. I always somewhere waited for that conversation to come up. And maybe, mayyyyybe, even thought that we could end up together. Like, together, together. And now, well now that…well, that is totally off the table, I find that I am what? A little disappointed? Noooo! Really? Disappointed? Yeah, I have to admit that I kind of am. Hmm….never saw that coming. Or did I?

Okay, now the lie that has to be invented. Why am I so upset with Aarav? What could he have done to make me upset with him but not so much that my parents would stop letting him come over.

Good thing is that I have always been quite a good inventor. Sometimes, I come up with stuff that is even more believable than the truth. Like this one right now.

'Ma, it's not like that, Aarav's my best friend and that's it.'

'Okay, then what is it?'

'Um...actually, there's this new boy in school, he's just come to our class. And I really like him.'

Mum stops her pacing, I can see that she's having a hard time processing that her little daughter is old enough to 'really like guys.' Really, Mom?

'Anyway, when I told Aarav this, he like really disapproved. He didn't want me to pursue this any longer. As though he is, I don't know, my keeper or something. I mean, who is he to say that I can talk to some guy or not?'

The speed of the lie amazes me. I'd be proud if I wasn't so ashamed.

My mum sits down. She has this really pleased expression on her face. I can see that all her reservations about Aarav have flown out the window.

She's not the only one out to control her boy-crazy daughter.

'I am sure he has some good reason to ask you to be careful,' Mum says triumphantly.

'Trust your best friend, apple pie,' says Dad, letting out a ball of stress that has obviously been choking him. 'At least you should allow him to express his reservations to you.'

'Yeah...I guess,' I can see they're super surprised that I've given in so easily. But I am not up for more conversation right now. I have a lot of stuff to process. So much in fact that my head is hurting and I think my heart is hurting even more. I can feel it hurting. I can feel my eyes blurring. I've got to get out of the room.

Next thing I know, I'm standing in front of my mirror. I've bunched my hair up into a baseball cap. I'm in my jeans and I've got a hoodie on. I'm trying to look like a boy. Would I ever do that? Would I ever even want to? Remotely? No, I cannot begin to imagine what that would be like. I am a girl. I was born a girl. And I will always be a girl. Of course, sometimes, when it comes to be allowed to stay out after dark, or come home in a cab alone, I have wished I was a boy instead. But that was more a convenience thing. Boys just seem to have it easier, is all.

And I would never actually want it. And I certainly would not in a thousand years do anything about it. It's like, when someone is being really, really irritating, you say, 'I want to kill you,' but you don't actually arm yourself and do anything about it, do you?

Then how come it's different with Aarav? I asked him if it was that he was gay. That's why he liked the new guy. Which, by the way, he had confessed to. He liked the new guy who I liked. IN the SAME way!

But that wasn't it. He seemed so sure. But how can one be sure of such a bizarre thing? It's just not natural. I mean, look, if he was just gay, I would be super cool with it. Okay, maybe not super cool at the beginning, but cool for now and super as soon as I had wrapped my head around it. But this, this was just crazy. Super crazy. Now and forever.

I have seen hijras on the streets. The ones who come begging, banging on your car window. Aggressive. Not like other beggars who will beg and plead. They're so scary. The hijras, I mean. And I've heard that they brutally cut off bits of themselves. The boy bits. How can they do that? Is....is Aarav thinking of something like that? The thought creeps me out so bad. I throw off the cap and yank off the hoodie. I want to be no one but myself. And right now, I want to just puke. And so I do. Puke. My stomach churns with dreadful thoughts. I almost puke my heart out. And afterwards, I feel no better.

How am I going to face him again? How will I look him in the eye? I know one thing. I'm going to have to be cool. No matter what I'm feeling inside, I'm going to have to hold it in. Because I do know that if all this is hard for me, then it's much, much harder for him. He's the one who is going to have to face the world with this. Does he even have a choice? I feel, right now, the best advice I can give him, if any, is to just lump it and not tell anyone else about this.

Maybe there are a lot of other people who have been born wrong. All kinds of wrong. But they just learn to live with it, right? If a person is blind, then they learn how to cope with that—they learn Braille, they get a white cane and whatever. But, basically, in most cases, they have to accept that their blindness is a permanent thing. I think that's what I'm going to tell him to do. Just accept that you're different. That's all. And that you're stuck with being different. That there is nothing you can really do about it.

I feel better now that I know what I'm going to say, how I'm going to face him.

*

But I felt worse once I said that to him. His face fell. It drained of colour and collapsed. It was as if someone had suddenly shrunk him. Like I'd shrunk him with my words that basically said, 'Just lump it, live with it.'

He turned on his heels and walked away. Without a word. Like I'd let him down and not understood a word. Which was true. I hadn't. I couldn't. How could I? Normal people aren't like this. I mean, have you ever met a hijra in real life? Been friends with one? Yeah, they are out there on the streets harassing people or storming into people's weddings and stuff and making a general nuisance of themselves. Would you ever invite one into your home? Voluntarily? Into your bedroom? Of course not. I am a pretty inclusive person, I am good to all kinds of people and mean to no one. But you have to draw the line somewhere. And hijras are my line.

I knew he'd hate that—being called a hijra. Being called a category of persons. He'd always hated that. That was one of the things I loved about him. I hung my head miserably. Love. The more I came to terms with the fact that I was never going to have a relationship with him beyond being buddies, the more I fell in love with him. This was the most painful thing I had ever been through in my life. In any case, I didn't even know what that made him. A eunuch, a transgender, a cross-dresser—what??

I googled it. There was so much information. About people who feel it and don't do anything, people who take hormones, people who surgically change themselves.

I had no idea. I felt so stupid, so ignorant.

I wished there was someone I could talk to. But the only one I could talk with was the only one with whom I couldn't. Life was so complicated. And suddenly, all the teen angsty complications seemed so insignificant. What was not being allowed to go for a movie in comparison to this? No comparision.

I called him. I thought maybe I have to do this over the phone. I could not face him right then. He could read my expressions awfully well.

He didn't take my calls. But I persisted. Eventually, he picked up with a gruff hello.

'Hi.'

Pause.

I could can hear the eggshells cracking metaphorically as we tried to walk over them.

The prepared speech went flying out of the window.

'What?'

'Just called to say "hey".'

Lame, I know, but it was the best I had.

Long pause got longer. Eggshells cracked some more.

'So you've said "hey". Anything else?'

'Aarav, I'm sorry, I'm really really sorry.'

'You are?'

'I am. I was stupid the way I reacted. I should have, I should have...'

'It's cool, don't worry about it. I don't know what else I expected. It was too weird for you to be okay right away, I should have got that too.'

'Whew...' I felt a gush of relief.

'Whew to you too,' he said, the relief huge for him too.

But then another awkward pause.

A 'where do we go from here?' kind of pause.

'How are you doing?' we said together. And started laughing. It was good to laugh, even though we both knew it is was an ineffective band-aid on a ginormous gaping wound. Or something like that.

'I…well…I honestly don't know how I'm doing. I'm freaked out, Aarav. I've never had to deal with anything like this before.'

Honesty is rarely my go-to best policy. But in this one case I knew that was the only card I had left to play.

'I know, I get it. I really do. But you know that I had to tell you. I mean, who else could I go to?'

'Yeah, but Aarav, dude, what are you going to do?'

I wanted to ask him a whole lot of questions about this. Like how long have you known and what in you feels like a girl and are you going to have a surgery or something. My mind was restless with questions, but I didn't know how to ask them. Because honestly, I didn't know if I was ready for the answers.

'Umm, I don't know, I mean, it's the first time I've actually spoken the words out loud…'

'To me?' Whoa, that was a load of responsibility on my shoulders.

'Yep.'

'Your parents?'

'Well, somewhere I think that they may know, or at least suspect something's amiss. But I haven't spoken to them, no.'

'So, you planning to, or just keep it between us?'

'No, I will. I will have to tell them. I can't live like this any longer. I feel, I feel that my life's nothing more than a lie.'

I could feel his heart breaking along with his voice.

'Wanna come over?'

'Listen, I don't think I can do this alone. Will you be with me when I tell them?'

I gulped. I didn't want to be there. I would literally rather be anywhere else on earth when my best friend told his parents that their son wanted to be their daughter instead.

'Sure, of course I'll be with you. Whatever you need.' I said with a mountain more confidence than I feelt.

'*Thanks...*'

His voice was small and sad. I could not begin to imagine what he was thinking. I could hardly figure out what I was thinking. What must he be going through? The courage it took for him to tell me. And we'd always shared literally everything.

But I have to do this. I will educate myself and then I will be there. He has to know that I have his back. I do. I will be his forever friend, because he needs me to be.

No, this isn't a blank page left by the printer by mistake. This isn't a mistake. This is what is called a writer's block. Or a lack of solution or resolution.

Because, honestly, this is just me now. Paro Anand. Not Aarav, not Saudamini or any food item.

Why?

Because Paro Anand cannot imagine what it must be like to be in Aarav's shoes. Or Saudamini's shoes. I've tried. I've spent sleepless nights. I know this is something some families face. But I do not know how a friend, especially a child, would react. How does someone like Aarav come to terms with finding that he is born into the wrong body? How does he come out into the world? This unforgiving world that casts aside people like him?

Oh, I've done my share of research and reading. And soul-searching. But I find that I cannot find myself in those shoes. And fitting into the shoes of the players in my story is an important, essential part of my writing. I can't do it otherwise. The issue of transgenders is a complicated one. There are a lot of technical, biological differences between different kinds of people of the broad group of transgenders. Too many for me to start describing here. If you are interested, there is information available. This is not the place for me to give it.

Then yesterday, I found myself face to face with a hijra. I was locked in the safety of my air-conditioned car. As I saw the group making their way at the traffic light, I found myself hoping that the light would change before one of them made their way to me. Most of us have felt that way, I think. It's true with most beggars, but with the hijras, there is an added fear.

But it wasn't to be. She knocked on my window. Not too aggressive. And, because I was writing this story, I decided to give her some money. It did not feel right for me to pretend to be asleep behind my sunglasses, which is what I usually do.

I reached into my wallet and pulled out what I thought was a generous hundred. I rolled down my window, making sure to lower it just a little bit (so she couldn't reach in and grab my wallet, as many of us have been told they do). She gave me a big smile. I smiled back and proudly handed the money. But of course, 'these people' are never satisfied with whatever they get, be it a tenner or a hunner. I tried to put my window back up but she knew I'd do that, so she had put her hand in and I almost squeezed her arm off by mistake.

But she was polite. She said she only wanted to bless me. So I offered the top of my head, feeling admittedly queasy.

She blessed me, she blessed my children as a five hundred note departed from my hand. The lights changed and I somewhere hoped that this little exchange of my trying to be a better human being would unlock the block.

It didn't. It hasn't. There is no way for me to know how to stand in those shoes.

But it's a story that needs to be written. We have been taught to fear hijras, we abhor them, we try and keep them as far as possible from us. And they in turn are aggressive and obnoxious. We wonder why these able-bodied people don't work instead of begging for a living. Never once acknowledging that we don't give a transgender a job.

Is it our fault? Is it theirs?

I don't know. All I do know is that right now there isn't a solution. To their condition, our conditioning. Or to this story.

But I would love to one day be able to say that I was a better friend to someone like Aarav who found himself quite literally in no-man's land.

Until then. A blank page and a half-written story is the best I have to offer.

so, cinderella

So, Cinderella...now there's a witch, if you ever needed one. Though why would anyone need a witch, really?

I mean, look at her, all goody-two-shoes—well, one shoe. You know what happened to the other one in *that* story. But this isn't that story. Why thrash that one out again? Old Cin doesn't need any more bleeding hearts out there. She's had enough and will continue to have them too. Nothing much I can do about it. Or care enough to, anyway.

Me? Well, I'm one of those rare Cinderella haters.

Maybe there are just two of them in the world. Me and my sister. Okay, here goes, my intro. I'm one of the Ugly Sisters. Imagine that as an introduction. Think about that conversation, 'Hello, I'm Suman, I'm Gita, I'm Sita.' And 'Hellooo, I'm Ugly Sister No. 2.'

Now, put yourself in my shoes for a fraction of a minute. And my shoes are sensible ones—broad and with an arch and ankle support built in. Much more comfortable than the tiny glass slippery slipper variety. Just as well there's only one stupid cow who can fit into those. Anyway, this isn't a Reebok ad, but rather the opposite. It's not about beauty, but about the beast. Namely, moi. Me, the one and only Ugly Sister. Well, okay, not the one and only. But two and lonely. Yep, it is pretty lonely when the only other one who will hang out with you is Ugly Sister No. 1. See, the truth is, imagine going through life being called the Ugly Sisters. What a title. Like, no one knows us by our real names. UgSis is as close to an identity that we'll ever get. And the hippest... Or Number 1 and Number 2 which is even less flattering than the ugly tag. Grin grin, wink wink.

Anyway, back to the story at hand. Cinderella and the ball. And we know who got the prince.

I know all of you have been brought up on the soppy drivel that paints us out to be the evil uglies who wouldn't let the darling Cinderella go to the party. It's like, if you're ugly, you're necessarily evil. Or if you're evil, you're ugly. They are synonyms. And that's not fair. And fair is not always lovely.

I can say for myself here, I was born ugly but I wasn't born evil. I was a kind, sweet, cheery girl who made her dad laugh as they played gentle pranks on her mother and elder sister. Elder sister was less looker and more shocker. I could see it in people's eyes when they saw her. Well, okay, us. When they saw us, there was a look of 'oh my god, where did that creature crawl out of?' on their faces.

And for a while it was okay. I accepted that that's how people reacted when they saw us. Because both of us were not only not pretty, we were far, far from it. Like a land far, far away. At home, it was fine, we enjoyed dressing up and throwing on Mum's clothes and begging for make-up which we would slather on. In truth, we weren't even just plain. That would have been okay, really. We were weirdly but not wonderfully UGLY. But we were fine. We were in the same boat, the same ugliness formed us both. And we didn't let it define us.

Then, when little Cin was born, we loved her dearly and we were not jealous. We played with her, looked after her. And helped Dad and Mum any way we could. Which wasn't a lot, because we were little and by little, I mean, really really little.

Yep we were the little people. I don't mind using the politically incorrect term 'dwarf' here. My sister and I are dwarves. Strange arms and big heads. People stare at us, some laugh behind their hands and think that we can't see that they are laughing at us. Somehow, people seem to think that if we are 'special need' then we must be blithering, blind idiots too who cannot see the smirks and sniggers and horrified expressions on their faces. Often, they don't even bother to hide their expression, because they probably assume that we are incapable of understanding what their raised eyebrows and dropped jaws mean.

We look at ourselves in shop windows where the mannequins sneer down at us, clearly saying that they have no clothes to fit our strange, misshapen bodies. For the longest time, well into our teens, our only option was to buy clothes in the kiddie section of clothing stores. Until one day we rebelled. We no longer wanted to be dressed in pink bows and frilly frocks. So Mum found a tailor who tried his best to adapt the clothes we pointed out from fashion magazines. The experiment wasn't always successful, but he did try so we didn't complain too much. And of course, we still had to shop for shoes in the kiddie section where the choices were either sturdy sneakers or fluffy pink shoes. We chose the former.

For the longest time, we even stopped eating out at restaurants because the waiter would helpfully bring baby high chairs. Which would actually have been useful, if they hadn't been embarrassing. And hurtful even. I mean, in truth, we couldn't reach the table from our chairs. But we were too old for baby high chairs. I remember, for a while we'd have fun with it. We'd behave like bratty babies, banging our spoons and slinging food at each other. It made Dad laugh and embarrassed Mum, which was the best combination. But after a while, as our faces matured and it was obvious we weren't infants, it became unbearably embarrassing. So we simply stopped going out. We would order food in and sit at our own table in our own version of baby high chairs. Without people staring and sniggering.

Anyway, so back to Cin. Of course, her name wasn't Cinderella. Our parents were not that weird or that mean that they would name the pretty daughter Cinderella because she had two ugly sisters. In any case, I think there has probably been only one Cinderella in the history of the world. But that's what my sister and I called her. To her face. Behind our parents' back. It was such a perfect fit. Cinderella and her monster ugly sisters.

Okay, I know I am sounding bitter, but you've got to have some sympathy here. I mean, she was really pretty. Beyond pretty. As she grew up, she became downright beautiful. She had these cherubic curls that softly framed her face and big, soft eyes that melted the hardest heart. And pink cheeks on a fair, fair face. She could be a model for fairness creams like Fair and Lovely. Her arms and legs were sinewy and long as though all my mother's length had been given to the one last sister, robbing us of normal-sized limbs.

Our sister Zara just seemed innocently unaware of the differences between her and us. She wasn't being silly, it's just that she was infuriatingly good. Like one of those silly, perfect fairy-tale princess types. All she needed was a cloud of rainbow butterflies fluttering around her adorable head and the picture would have been perfect.

And we, her ugly dwarves. Yep, she was Cinderella and we the ugly sisters. She was Snow White and we were her two dwarves. And no matter how annoying it was, she loved us. As she grew taller, she would help us reach for stuff, care for us. Which was all the more galling—after all, we were supposed to be her elder sisters.

As she started going to school with us, we could see the question on everyone's faces. The same face which said, 'Eh? How come?' What could we answer? We didn't know. Our parents didn't know—we asked them what had happened.

See, we don't even have many friends. Even the fellow uglies don't want to hang out with other uglies. It's like it's contagious. And no one wants to catch ugliness. Not even the pre-ugly people. The Beast wanted to hang out with the Beauty, the old bearded dwarves got all soft on Snow White. It was probably only the politically correct Shrek who preferred the big green chick over the delicate little princess. And, in any case we do know how the prince reacted when he saw the flip side of his beauteous princess. It's not a question of right and wrong. It's just how it is.

And have you noticed? The uglier you are, the

meaner, the stingier, the rottener you are. And conversely, the prettier you are, the more likely you are to be kind, loving, giving and that lot of adjectives. At least in fairy tales. But even in real life, the uglies have to be extra talented or extra kind to get a pass beyond their dreadful looks. Like in our Sanskrit textbook in school, there's this conversation between a white swan and a black cuckoo. I'll share a direct translation:

Cuckoo: You are so white, therefore you are so beautiful, therefore people love you.

Swan: Although (yep, the actual word is yadyapi *and it translates literally to 'although') you are black, you have a sweet voice, therefore people love you also.*

Get my point? The swan needs no extra talent or anything because of its colour. Fair equals lovely. And lovely equals love and popularity. However, the cuckoo must sing to compensate for its blackness! As though the black feathers denote a black heart that can be forgiven only by melodious song. What really gets me though, is the irritating benevolence in the Swan's tone. Like, she (it's got to be a she, the he's don't have it so bad, I think, though I can't honestly say for sure), so she never once says, 'No, no, my white feathers mean nothing. I am not so loved, actually, because I have a mean bite and a horrendous honk.' She just accepts the fact that her fairness makes her beautiful which in turn makes her lovable. Biting and honking notwithstanding.

In real life, though, it's mostly the pretty girls who are also the mean girls. They will gang up against us uglies, and make us feel fat, stupid, short. And smelly and covered in lice and stuff. The uglies don't have the guts, mostly, to be the mean ones. They would rather stay out of the spotlight. Look around you. Look in any group. The prettiest girl will be the leader, the one who calls the shots. And those shots are almost always directed at the less pretty ones.

Don't be an ostrich, pull your head out of the sand, you know it's true.

See, you've got to see it from our point of view. Okay, I agree, in the fairy tale, the sisters kept Cin out, tried to make sure she couldn't go to the prince's ball because she was dirty. But also because under all that cinder we knew that she was this pretty, fragile delicate kind of chick who guys somehow really go for. They like to pretend that they are the only ones who can protect the sad, fragile girl. They are actually threatened by good, solid girls like us. See, we don't need protection. We can manage ourselves perfectly well. Well, unless there's something that we need on a high shelf or something. And if push comes to shove, we will do our share of pushing and shoving to protect our guy. But instead of being grateful for it, guys just feel threatened. They weren't man enough to protect themselves and the girl they happened to be with when the pushing and shoving began. But honestly, they aren't man enough to admit that sometimes, it is okay for a girl to step up. Even if it's a small step by a little person.

My sister and I, the ugly twosome, had a long time ago decided that we were going to tough it out. We were going to manage and if we couldn't, we would do without. And we more or less did that. The school had a special toilet built for us and the wash basin was lowered so we could wash our hands. We had special desks which went with us to the next class. So all was pretty okay. Even if we weren't pretty. Okay?

But guys prefer helpless girls to ones who make the best of a bad case of dwarfism. I know plenty of girls who are able to cross a busy road all by themselves, sensibly and safely. They do it on a regular basis. But if there is a boy on the horizon, they suddenly turn into a puddle of helplessness, shrieking and holding onto any available arm or hand. And the guy? Well, the guy positively puffs up with manly pride and probably a few more chest hairs pop up under his shirt in sheer glee. He escorts the helpless girl across the road and does not let go of her hand even once they are safely across. In short, Zara types.

And somehow, he does not notice me crossing the very same road. Even if Pretty Girl can run twice as fast as I can on her long, or normal-sized legs. Probably he's thinking that it may not be a bad thing if I do get run over by a truck or something. Or am I just overreacting? I think I would probably fall if some poor jerk took my arm to help me across the road. From shock. I mean, I'm super short. But I am not super helpless.

I don't know why I'm going on and on about crossing roads, when it has nothing to do with anything. I have no roads to cross anyway. I am, in fact, standing at a dead end. So why am I talking about crossing roads? Well, I guess I am trying to give you the correct image of Cin as opposed to us, Ugly Number 1 and 2.

And then, there was a party. It was thrown by the most popular boy in school. Possibly the richest one too. I mean, a real catch. He had invited the whole school, it seemed. At least senior school. He was also a really cute guy and everyone, including the two of us, had huge crushes on him. He pretended not to notice most girls. And he actually didn't notice us at all. But he did invite us. Which was great. Except that he also invited our taller, fairer, pretty, long-limbed sister. It's entirely possible that he invited us so that he could invite our sister who was in a junior class. She was, after all, the only one from her class who was invited.

'This is it, this is the ball the prince is having and he is going to choose our Cinderella. Any bets?'

'Yeah, let's not take her, let's just lock her up in the attic.'

'Stupid, we don't even have an attic.'

'And if we did, we wouldn't be able to reach it.'

And so, the ugly sisters and Cinderella arrived at the prince's party.

We got a fair panic attack of the Dark and Uglies. I mean, the prince had invited ALL the girls of high school. Really, ALL the women? What did he think we were? A buffet spread out for him to pick and choose and try one dish after the other? Well, come to think of it, that's probably what he did think.

Honestly, we all should not have complied. It would have served him right if none of us arrived and he had this big party with empty dishes. Or something. But that NEVER ever happens, as we all know. Mothers and aunts were sweating with excitement as they all rushed to the shops, sparing no expense this time around, whether it was clothes or shoes or bags or jewellery, it was designer, designer, designer all the way. And pretty soon, girls were tarting it up at beauty saloons (yeah, salooooons not salons with a French accent, though there were those as well. I mean, remember, he wanted to give the once over to ALL the chicks. The ones who went to salooooons and the ones who went to salons.)

The buffet was abuzz with delicious chicks and tarts (oooh, I know I am going to get into trouble for this one. It is just sooo politically incorrect.)

And we were there too. In our ill-fitting, over-tight, very corseted outfits, having stuffed our oedema-ed feet into heels higher than our pelvic girdles could support. Each one of us pretending to smile at friends old and new, though wishing we could actually put a few out of action.

Again, the fair and lovely ones were standing in the middle of the room, and us hanging about, close to being wallflowers. They were giving us the snidest sniggers that clearly said, 'Why have you bothered to come here? You don't stand a chance in hell!' which, sadly, was true. My sister and I were not even the also rans. And heart of hearts, we knew that we were no queen of hearts.

Why had we come? Was a flicker of hope kindling somewhere deep inside of us? Were we really hoping that the words those drop-dead gorgeous beauty queens say at beauty pageants that it's the beauty within that matters and not what's on the outside? That, we all knew was a load of crap at most times. But most especially at this time, this moment. This sad, sad right here and now.

So instead, we gorged ourselves on the snacks that were going around and clapped our hands as if we were enjoying the bawdy songs being sung by some bold piece of a girl (who was never going to be picked either. She was too brassy and bold and for sure the prince was only going for the simpering, helpless ones) and as the evening wore on, the field had obviously narrowed down to five or six girls.

There was music. There was a dance floor. And there were more girls than boys. At first I was sad about that because I had thought, if not prince charming, maybe one of the other boys would ask me. Where had all the other boys gone? Who was going to be doing the dancing? And then it struck me. Wow. This was going to be the best party ever. See, I loved to dance. Like truly. But whenever I went to a party, I had to wait demurely in a corner, waiting for some guy to come up and ask me to dance. I mean, what's with that? Do I need permission to dance? Does a random guy have to give me that permission? And if I were to just jump onto the dance floor and start to dance, well, the sniggering would drown out the music. Women don't dance alone. Why not, I would want to scream. As I waited. And waited. And waited. But you knew that already, didn't you?

But now, here at the prince's party, since there were not enough guys, we could just start dancing, right? Right? No? Nope. Nobody else was dancing at all.

There was tension in the air that was thick and stewy. Like a vile brew cooking in a witch's cauldron. We girls were milling around. Pretending to be polite with, 'Hello, how are yous' and 'long time no sees' peppering the air. Along with fake compliments about how gorrrgeous someone looked.

You could tell which ones were fake by the excessively long-drawn-outness of some words. Gorrrrrgeous. Loooovely. Sooooo good to seeee you. We all knew it was fake. And we were well aware, most of all, that we were in fact competing with each other and were hoping we were at least prettier than the next one. The buzz grew louder and then suddenly fell silent. Like when a teacher walks into an unsupervised classroom. And we all turned around. There were eyes and words only for one person now. Well, two people. Party boy had asked his Cinderella—our Cinderella—to dance.

Prince had come in. He looked pretty cute and he was polite enough to come up to each of us and say thanks for coming. I almost melted when he held my hand. That is, until he patted it in a brotherly sort of way. Oh wait, was that brotherly or pityingly? I know that look, I've known it all my life. And the only way I could hold myself up on my legs was to think that what he had done was give me a brotherly pat and not a pity pat. If only I could dance, I'd show him that there was something worthwhile in me. But instead, the few boys went up to the many girls and asked a handful to dance. While we just stood there. Rooted like trees on our fat stumps. I was a great dancer. Not like these simpering pretty ones who shifted their weight from one foot to another in a bad imitation of what a dance should not look like. I mean, pathetic. But I stood and I watched. Plastered a smile on my face and pretended as hard as I could pretend. Wearing my best, 'I only came here to stand about and watch others make a fool of themselves. I didn't come here to dance. Much less to be chosen by any dumb prince.' Right. I felt bitter and so I sound bitter.

I stole a glance at the others who were also rooted here, wallflowers all. We smiled at each other, each one feeling a common pain and embarrassment. There was precious little that I could do. Somehow, it was so desperate that we couldn't even offer any comfort to each other. We were all in the very same, very leaky boat, but we couldn't say to each other, 'Look, we're never going to get chosen, so let's forget about the dumb prince and just have a blast. Let's eat the snacks and kick our shoes off and dance like no one is watching us.' Although, of course, the only time anyone would be watching us was if we were a bunch of girls dancing and laughing and having an uproariously, inappropriately good time. You know the kind of sniggers that would happen then. So we just stood there. Sad, rooted, hopeless trees lining the walls of a ball.

All right, I admit. I want this story to go like a fairy tale. Like a proper 'happily ever after' one. One where hope springs and all ends in a bright shiny place. Where a medium good-looking, medium tall dude comes up and asks me for a dance. Oh it could be anyone. I know not to aim as high as the prince himself. I will take anyone. Literally.

But no one came. Not that night. Yes, Cin did. She arrived. Of course not in a pumpkin carriage with rats for horses. Just an ordinary Ola. And yes, the prince was swept off his feet and yes, the clock struck midnight and we all had to go home. But not after Cin had flung off her too tight, too high heels and danced like mad. And yes, I'll even admit that she dances pretty well. And yes, she couldn't find one of her shoes in all that crowd. So Ugly Sisters 1 and 2 had to almost carry her down the stairs and into our car where she sat moonily in the back seat while I sat in front with the driver.

We got home and I felt so miserable. I was kicking myself as I slid back into comfy flip flops that I had gone at all. Ugsis 1 had not said a word all evening, at least in the car and then she had stormed into her room in her flouncy dress and slammed the door shut.

I looked around at Cin. She was still in her pretty dress, smile plastered on her mug and you could see the stars in her eyes. She was the one who was going to be getting the prince. Some fairy tales never change. I stood in front of her, struggling with the zipper of my dress, but unable to reach because it was too tight. And my arms were too short.

She didn't even notice my troubles and instead, drew hearts in the dust on the coffee table. Did she really not have a clue as to how hard this was for us, her very own sisters? Was she really that blind that she was so blissfully unaware of the heartache we went through? Had she not bothered to notice that we had not danced all night?

I ripped my dress as I struggled out of it. Good. I was never going to wear it again. Hateful thing. I held it in my hand for a fleeting moment, then, without another thought, I bunched it up like a giant duster and wiped the stupid dust hearts off the table. Cin looked up at me surprised and hurt. Tears springing to her large, sad eyes clearly saying, 'How could you?'

'Why...?' she said, in her little girl voice that set my teeth even more on edge.

'WHY? WHY? You really want to ask me WHY??'

The real tears rolled down her peachy pink cheeks. 'But what did I do?'

And it's true. Of course, she didn't DO anything. Except be Cin, well, Zara...of course, she couldn't help it. But she needed to know. Someone needed to tell her.

And I was going to be that someone. We sat up all night, almost. And I told her how the two of us felt left out. How the world made us feel so ugly and unwanted. Most of the time, she sat as though turned to stone. Except to munch on the popcorn we made because, delicate pretty thing had not eaten at the party, because delicate pretty things are not supposed to eat. And that was a revelation too. That there were rules and strictures on them as well. That the pretties had to behave by a certain code just as much as the uglies did. That the pretty ones really hated each other because they were the real competition. At least we lot hung about like a herd, the pretty ones were on their own. No packs for them. And most of all, they had to pretend to never be hungry, never take a bite of the food, no matter how good it smelled. Hmm, okay, this was news to me. I guess there was pressure on the pretties to remain so. But honestly, it was nothing compared to the uglies trying to knock on the pretty door. But, I get now that everything may not be easy and golden behind that door either.

Hang on. I am not going to be a sudden convert to sympathizing for the 'other side'. Not at all. I mean, I would take those troubles over mine in a minute. There was no comparison. See, she could come home and eat popcorn and get the guy and everything. The tasty party snacks were only going to take me so far. And no further.

I'd rather be a starving pretty than a well-fed ugly. I'd rather squeeze my feet into glass slippers and dance in them no matter how much they hurt than wear comfy shoes, no matter how much I could stride comfortably in them.

But all right, we are different. And just as Cin was never going to be an ugly, no matter how hard she tried (although, yeah, why would she try?) I had to come to terms with the fact that I was going to be a bit weird all my life and never cross over to the other side. Like it or not, here I am. And some day I am going to fall in love with my own Prince Notsocharming. And he is going to be pleased to have a good sturdy wife and I am going to...well, I don't know what else I am going to be. And here, I'd like a drumroll please because this is my big realization. If Notsocharming doesn't appear, I'm good with that too. I am quite, quite capable of living a fulfilling life all on my own.

I don't know much. But I do know, that come what may, I am going to be happy.

inner circle, outer circle

The circle turns and tightens, and we all stand. Watching.

Our blood turns cold, freezing. It boils, thumping in our ears. And we all stand. Watching.

Our hands clench into fists. But our feet grow solid roots. And we stand here. Watching.

The screams go on, the cries for help. But we just stand here. Watching.

Rooted to the spot, frozen into impotence. But I just stand there. Watching.

I want someone to make a move. If someone

else moves forward to save her, I will too. But no one moves forward. No one stretches out their helping hand.

I hear the screaming.

'Bachaaao!' a moan. Or is it a whisper? A cry for help or a whisper for help.

It's coming from her as her yellow sari turns to brown as the sari is lifted to expose her legs. Bare. Naked.

Help. Help. Me.

Is it her?

Is it me?

Have I cried out?

I move. I must move. I must. Someone must. And if no one else does, then it has to be me. As I move forward I hope that someone else is going to join me. I am scared witless, but my feet know where to go. I think I am screaming. I know I am flailing my arms. Hoping that there are others who will see me move and know that if everyone gets together, we can beat the living daylights out of these thugs. Or at the very least, get them to run away. And save the girl. That's all I want to do. Save the girl.

Alone, I can't do anything, but together we can. We must.

As I reach them, screaming at the top of my voice, flailing my arms, one of them turns to look at me. His eyes are fiery, his mouth is slack with shock. He didn't expect anyone to come. But they've stopped hitting her. They are looking at me. Why are they grinning?

I scream for help.

At first no one comes. One of the men gets to his feet. He asks if I want the same treatment. He points at the sobbing girl at his feet. He asks if I would like the same. But just as he reaches out for me,

A shoe

Comes flying

And hits

Him.

Unbalanced, he turns in a fury. But there is a wall of onlookers. Who are tired of being onlookers. They have turned into do-ers. And their arms are raised. And they—We—We have a rage of our own. We are not going to turn a blind eye. We are sick of blind eyes. I have always been taught, in school and at home to stick up for the one who is vulnerable, to step forward and right a wrong. That justice is doing the right thing. We are all taught that. And we are sick of our own impotence. We are going to stop them. Right now. They are a small bunch compared to the strength of our numbers. And we have a violence within. We are willing to use it. At last. At last we know that compassion means action.

The girl disappears in the ruckus. Probably caught a bus or auto. She does not want her face splashed across TV screens and social media. She is embarrassed of what we might have seen of her. I can understand that. And after a tiny twinge of annoyance that she didn't even turn and thank me for being so brave, I see it from her point of view. She would have had to go to the cop station, confront these guys again. And who knows if her family would have shamed her, made her stay home, give up her job. Whatever. So I understand and I don't mind that she didn't acknowledge that I had just saved her life.

The police take the thugs away. And some small-time television news channel interviews me. I am a little bit of a celebrity, but I know that I couldn't have done it if the others had not stepped forward. If I had tried to save her on my own, I may well have become a victim myself.

But...

I move now. Restlessly tossing in my too hot bed. The screaming voice won't quiet down, the hitting and cutting, hitting, cutting,

hittingcuttinghittingcutting.

Some more. I move now, raising my arms, raising my voice, screaming my own screams. Until my mother comes running in, followed by my father who hovers by the door. Their lines of worry are louder in the stillness of the night. None of us sleep. None of us have. After that.

She was on her way to work, the young woman in a yellow sari. Just a regular day, probably wolfed down breakfast, grabbed a tiffin made by her mother. Or herself. Had her sari pallah caught on the door as she slammed it shut behind her, pulling her up short...

The images refine themselves at every pass. Sometimes, it's the colour of the sari. Sometimes, what's in the tiffin box. Her gasp as she finds her sari is caught. The irritation as she re-opens the door to free her clothes.

Her mother calling out to her, asking why she came back. 'Kya hua? Sab theek to hai na?' insisting on knowing why she is still there on the doorstep.

'Oh ho, Ma, it's nothing.'

'Nothing? Then why are you still here, won't you be late?' You know how mothers can be. Can't leave a thing unanswered.

Did she answer? Did she stop to explain? If she had stopped, would it have been a bit different?

Or did her mother stand at the door, looking at her daughter's hurriedly retreating back, hand to her mouth, then turning back to the household chores that occupied her, thinking, 'Fine, I'll ask her again in the evening.'

Not knowing that there would be no one left to ask in the evening. That very evening. In just an hour or just a few minutes, even. There would be no one left to ask. But the mother had no moment of impending doom or a foreboding that made her call out to her daughter to say, 'Listen, just stay home today, skip your work, tell them you're sick. Something terrible is going to happen today.' Hindsight is cheap. It plays tricks on you. But afterwards. After words. Long after there are no words left.

If the mother did or didn't do any of these things, I would not know, for I wasn't there. I didn't know her. Or her family. But I can't help the images and thoughts that play through my brain, through my sleep. Clearly. As if I knew them and was there.

But I wasn't there. I was on my way to school, walking along, unmindful of the people who passed me by, dodging dog poo and spit puddles on the road. Keeping my head down like a good girl. Books held firmly across my chest like a shield. Because, yes, I was a warrior. A warrior for having chosen school over staying at home. And my books were going to be my weapon of choice. And so, I hugged them to my chest so that my chest looked ironboard flat and did not tempt any passing leery man to casually put his claw out and grab without mercy. Me crying out in pain, and then shushing it up as others looked at me, almost grinning, wondering, did I like it. *Like it*? Are you crazy? It's painful and humiliating. And I can't even put my hand up and caress the soreness because who could caress their breasts in public? And so I clutched my shield of books and kept my head down as I headed to school, unmindful of those I passed.

Did she protect herself with something across her chest? Was she a warrior? Yes, she was. She fought. And if we had all stepped forward, she would have been a warrior still.

But I have never been taught, in school, at home, to stick up for the one who is vulnerable, to step forward and right a wrong. That justice is doing the right thing. None of us has been taught that. Instead, we are taught to protect our own skins, to look out for ourselves. And we may be sick of our own impotence. But we were never going to stop them. Yes, we are sick of our blind eyes, but we don't open our eyes, we don't raise our arms up to stop that injustice. Even though she screams out. Bachaao. And whimpers, help me, help me. We turn deaf ears. Blind, deaf, mute. That's us. That's me.

And so, she may have been a warrior. But there was no fight left in her. I watched the light go out, the fight go out.

They came from out of nowhere. I think. At least it was nowhere for me. I was busy looking down, not meeting any eyes. Being my own little warrior, in my own little world.

But they caught her, not bothering about the other people crowding around. They were confident that this was a crowd of impotents. A crowd of inaction. Not that there was anything special about this crowd. No, it was a crowd pretty much like any other crowd in this city. They knew no one was going to step forward to help her. And no one did. Not one of us. Us. Yes, me.

The attackers were not bothered that it was early in the morning, that there were temple bells that had just rung, an azaan just sung. A time for seeking blessings for a good day ahead. A time for going about one's business. And *this* was their business? Is *this* what they did for a living? They stealthily pushed through the milling crowd and cornered her as she was about to step off the kerb and cross the road.

They caught her right across the road from me. I heard the scream. And then everything seemed to slow down. Like the scream had altered time, thickened it, muddied it.

They caught her right in front of the crowd and they yanked her off the road by her hair. I saw the feet go out from under her. Saw a chappal fly towards the road as though it knew it was supposed be crossing. With or without her. It came flying towards me. Was it asking me for help? I watched it rise. I watched it fall. I watched.

They caught her as she fell and then they fell upon her too. The sari, yellow, turned colour as it disappeared to reveal legs. Bare and long and kicking and fighting. Kickingfighting.

I stood rooted. Across the street. It was as if the world stopped turning. Like someone had shouted

'STATUE' and everyone turned to stone. Except that everyone was looking at the firestorm of movement. There was no sound except the hitting, screaming, cutting.

Everyone stopped in their tracks. Those who were rushing to get wherever they had to now seemed in no hurry at all. They had nowhere else to be except here, watching a woman, or was she a girl, being stripped naked, being hit, being cut. Being assaulted. I cannot bring myself to say it...she was being assaulted in every which way...in every way that a woman can be assaulted.

Even from way across the road I could see it. And I watched.

I think I took one step forward. But I am not sure that I actually did. And I think someone held my arm and shook their head, telling me not to go forward. But I am not sure there was anyone who did that. I have thought about those moments so many times over and over that I may have put in details of things that I think may have happened. Or things that I wish had happened. Things that I wish I had done.

Like trying to stop them. Or at least taking that one step forward to put an end to the horror that was happening. But I am not sure I did. I don't think any one of us took that one step forward in an attempt to stop it. And so no one put their arm out to stop me from taking the risk. No one needed to. I never took that first step either.

And the horror is that the attackers well knew that we would not. Take a step. Raise a hand. Raise a voice. Nothing. We stood like a block of Nothing. Watching.

They violated her. They hit her. And yes, they killed her. One knife wound at a time. One slash, one scream, one gasp, one whimper, one whisper at a time. Silence. Nothing.

I didn't move then. I watched. Along with everyone else. And since then I am trying to convince myself that after all, I am just a child. If none of the grown-ups standing there could do anything, I couldn't either, right? Right. Of course right. I could hear all the warnings of my father. 'We are sending you to school though everyone is warning us of the many dangers to young girls. Don't get into any trouble now. If you see trouble, stay away. It has nothing to do with you.'

Was it these words of warning that kept me away? Or was it my cowardice? I don't know. I don't know. I fear it was the second, it was cowardice that froze me from the inside out. But now, in the middle of the night, as I thrash myself awake, the movement won't stop. I want to, need to take that step. To make it count. To save that girl or woman in the yellow sari. To stab out, lash out at the men who pulled her off the road as her chappal flew forward and put an end to all her journeys. One knife wound at a time.

My father holds me tight in his arms. As he strokes my hair, wet with sweat and fear, he rocks me as I whisper.

'Did I do right, Papa? You told me to stay out of trouble and I did, Papa. I wanted to say something, do something, stop something. But I didn't. Was I right or was I wrong, Papa?'

I want him to say I was right. I want him to say I was wrong.

He is silent. And then he stops rocking me. He stops stroking my head. He has become very still.

I don't know what he is thinking. I become still too. What is he going to say?

'I'm sorry, it's my fault. I should not have told you to stay out of trouble, no matter what. But I take that back now. Next time, step forward, make a noise. Be

a voice that matters. Next time, don't be afraid. You can be the first voice of protest. And once there is one, there will be others.'

Is this what he wants to say? Is this what I want to hear? Would I have the courage to follow his advice now?

'It's sad very sad that this happened. I wish there had been someone who would have stepped up. But, beta, I can't advise that you be the first. I can't tell you to put yourself in danger. Eventually, you have to protect yourself first.'

But he doesn't say that either. I know that this too is not what I want to hear. But this is the advice I had followed.

'Papa,' I plead, 'what's right, what's wrong? I don't know which way is right. I don't know. Papa, tell me what to do.'

He looks at me, straight into my eyes. I try and tell him what's burning in my heart.

'Papa, we were so many and they were just a handful. If we had all stepped forward, we could have stopped them. We could have saved her.' My voice breaks. 'She would still be alive if we had all got together and helped her.

'What should I have done, Papa? Because doing nothing feels very, very wrong.'

He sighs finally and he holds my shoulders. 'You are right. Doing nothing feels wrong. Because it is wrong. You are right, wise one!' We smile.

'Then what...?'

'Well, I can't tell you to put yourself in danger, of course. I just can't, I'm your father. But maybe you can tell people around you that you should all start shouting. And you can call the police. Call the women's helpline, what is it?'

'1091, I think.'

'Yes. And 100 which is the police number. Call them. Tell them your location. Even carefully try to film the attack so that they can be identified, but be careful for your own safety. And if there are a few people who will shout with you, create a commotion. Then others will join in too. It's just a distraction, but it may be enough.'

'Papa, I could start a campaign on social media. Getting people to start shouting if something bad is happening. And it can become a movement. Something like the #MeToo movement. There must be a lot of people who want to do something, but don't know what and are too scared. Like I was.'

'We can call it the "Shout out Loud" or "Shout for Peace" project,' says Ma. She is standing by the door. And she is smiling. We are all smiling. Smiling after a long, long time.

I know it's not going to bring back the girl in the yellow sari. But I will put a yellow banner in her honour. That will be the logo. Or something. I know it's not much. But at least it's something. I cannot be on the silent outer circle anymore.

grief (is a beast)

Grief is a heavy beast who sits on your chest and bends your shoulders. Down. Grief is a beast who whispers un-words into your mind and paralyses you. Grief is a beast who will slip through your spine, unravelling it so that you cannot stand up straight and tall anymore. Grief is a beast.

I am too young for this. To feel like this. But Grief—and I use the capital because it is a beast—a being that is more real than father or mother or brother who can be small-lettered. Almost all the time. But not Grief.

Grief is too heavy a beast for my very young shoulders. It may be okay for when you are older, but Grief's too big for my size. Yet, here it is, claws and jaws and eyes that bind you into stillness. Into silliness. I am too young to be so still.

Yet here I sit, unmoving, for there is enough movement all around me. A whirling of dervishes who will not stop. Someone is getting flowers, someone is arranging them into shapes that are supposed to be pretty or soothing. But they are not. The smell of them is the smell of the beast. I will never love the smell of marigold again. The smell. Sweet. Coming cloying into my mouth and nose and choking the life out of me. But I am still, and I cannot move my hand to shut off my nostrils. I have never been so still before. Not even in my sleep. For there the dreams will move me. But now my brain is stilled into a stupor, there are no thoughts, no buzzing connections being made from one neuron to another. Except maybe the ones that make me breathe. I want, desperately, to lie down awhile. But my brain won't read my heart, so my muscles don't get the instruction. If I were to move it would be because I had fallen down or been pushed. Grief is my shroud even as they draw the shroud over my mother. My Mother.

Someone taps me on the shoulder, telling me to be brave. But I don't know what is expected of a person when they are being brave. Am I to take up arms and fight a battle? Am I to fight with someone? Stand in front of a speeding car and try and stop it with my bare hands? I look at my hands. They are so empty. I have no cards left to play. No tricks up these sleeves of mine. The only thing that I can do is to keep holding my mother's hand. As though I will never let go. Her cold, cold hand. It does not hold me back. The only thing I can do is to not let them take her. When the time comes.

The time has come.

There is nothing more that I can do to keep my mother here. They will be taking her away. And that will be that. And after a while, these whirling dervish people will be gone and I will be left to my stillness. My existence within the void that I am in. The void that is within me. For I feel myself to be a big, dark, tubular hollow. As though whatever was there has been dug out and a giant gaping hole filled with a gluey mass of nothing is all that is left.

Someone says to me, 'I'm sorry you lost your mother,' and somehow, I almost laugh out loud. For a horrible moment, I think I grin because the face of the person who is standing in front of me pales and there is confusion there. I must have grinned. A voice inside of me wants to get out and say, 'I've not lost her, silly, you make it sound as if I've misplaced her somewhere, the way she was always misplacing her glasses. As though I've lost her in a way that I may even find her again. I've not lost her. She's dead.'

I quell the voice. I straighten my face, I almost apologize for the smile, but all I do is to meekly nod my head and acknowledge the condolence.

I dig deep. Deeper than I have ever gone within myself and I try and hunt for some slight light. A sliver of silver. I know I am trying to be clever with words, to try and find something to make you smile. Or make me smile. Or something. But there is no silver, no sliver, no light. And certainly no smile. So how do I find my way? Which direction should I head towards?

I try to distract myself—fill my mind with thoughts of food. It is nauseating. Someone brings me a plate of someone else's food. Food from another, unknown kitchen. A kitchen that doesn't know that I don't like garlic in my food, and tomato skins have to be removed from the curry, or I gag on them. But the fires of our home are stilled too. No fragrance of frying onions, no wafts of cinnamon tea.

There will be no mother-cooked food again. Ever. Oh the home fires will start, salt will be sprinkled, onions will fry. But always by other hands. Never by mother hands.

There I go again, trying feebly to be clever with words. Like band-aids on raw skin. They won't allow the wounds to heal. But I keep putting them there anyway. And then pulling them off.

I have to get these words out of the way. For they are choking me. Or something is choking me, I am not really sure. Well, no, I am sure. It is this big, hairy ball of Grief that sits in my throat so that I cannot cough it up. Will I ever breathe free again?

*

A month, or is it two? Am I breathing? Am I whole again?

No. More hole than whole. The emptiness grows like a black hole eating into the light and laughter.

Oh, on the outside I can smile, even laugh. A little. On the outside I nod my head at someone who talks to me, and double up with laughter when someone cracks a joke. Double up, yes.

Because then no one will know that I'm not really laughing. My head between my knees, laughter-like sounds escaping my lips. And in my head, there are instructions going towards my heart, saying, 'Buckle up, cover up. Don't let them know, don't let them know.'

And mostly, no one does. This is a pain that no one can know until it hits them smack in the face. So no, don't tell me to be brave. Don't tell me that enough time has passed and I should pull myself together.

I am pulled together. Tight. Wound up. Wounded up. Still. And I may just be for a long, long time to come. The calendar can record time lapsed. In my heart time is frozen. Thicker, slower. Like sludge.

*

But then comes a time when I start to look around and start to notice things that are happening around me. They have probably been happening all this time. But I didn't have the eyes to see.

The lump in my throat shrinks. A bit. Till it is no longer too painful to swallow. Ever so slightly at first, so I have not noticed it.

There is no light yet, but the darkness is not so

dense anymore. Maybe I can swim upwards at last. I watched a television show in which there were these people talking about going to a shrink and how it had really helped them get over stuff. Whatever their stuff was.

A shrink? Did I need one of those? If I were to suggest it to anyone in my family, they would have a heart attack and I'd be back in front of a funeral pyre. Mental health is not an issue in our family. We are more of a sweep it under a carpet, or better yet, under some heavy furniture and leave it to play with hairballs and dust bunnies down there kind of a family.

So, even though I am more and more convinced that I may need to talk to someone more professionally qualified than...than who? And that's when it hits me. I haven't really talked to anyone since it happened. I have blocked it out of all conversation. When my friends tried to condole...I probably shut them down, made it more awkward than it needed to be. So then they didn't try anymore. And some practically stopped hanging out with me much. I guess I was no longer fun. Who knows. I was too busy shutting everyone up and shutting everyone out to keep count. And so, I haven't talked to anyone.

I know now that Grief is a beast which feeds off silence. The more you keep inside, the more you feed the beast. Talking may have starved Grief, diminished it. I know that I need to get talking soon. I can't talk to Dad. He is so immersed in his own grief, I don't think I could possibly burden him with a slice of mine. Maybe he needs someone to talk to too. Maybe...maybe...

He is the only one I need to talk to. I wish Mum was here. She would be able to tell us what to do. She would be the one I could turn to and talk it out.

The only one.

Ha, but if Mum was here, Grief wouldn't and there'd be nothing to talk about. She was the one I did talk to, more than anyone. Whether it was the pain of a scraped knee, or the pain of a friend who had sneaked behind my back and told everyone a secret I had shared with her in trust. Mum was my go-to and there wasn't anyone else I had ever bothered about. When you have someone good at that, you don't look around for a spare, a back-up in case the first one fails. Or dies. So I never needed another go-to. Certainly not Dad. Did he have a go-to person? If there was anyone, it would have been

Mum too. They were really, really close. They were best friends. I had never thought of him needing someone to confide his troubles in, but I guess that is just childish. Of course he would have needed someone. Everyone does. Don't they? He must be struggling with this as much as I am. Could it be that he is struggling even more than I am? I mean, I do have my whole life ahead of me. I am going to go off to college, travel, hopefully maybe fall hopelessly in love and whatever. But he? He had his one true love. And she is gone. And he would not know where to even start to find another. Even a friend or a companion. What is he going to do with his life ahead? I shiver. I have been so lost in my grief that I didn't think that there was another living, grieving person right behind another door. Right in another living, breathing heart. There are two beasts here.

I'm standing in front of Dad's room now. His door is shut, as it's been a lot nowadays. I hadn't really thought about how shut-in he has been. I feel a pang of guilt and then diminish it with a 'well, I'm here now.'

I knock. There is silence on the other side. Maybe he's asleep?

Knock.

Wait.

Wait.

Knock.

'Who is it?'

The voice is so faint. He must have been asleep.

'It's just me...'

His 'Yes?' is formal, as if I am a hawker come to the door to sell something. I am, I am selling a shoulder to cry on, an ear to hear. But how do I tell him this? It sounds so corny. Besides, we've never done this before.

I look at him. He wasn't asleep. His hair is neatly combed. He is neatly, even crisply dressed. He was just shut in his room. He was just shut in. Like I was.

'Dad...?'

'You need something?'

'Just you,' I wanted to say, but instead I tried to smile at him.

Yes, Grief is a beast. And I think it's here to stay. But here I am, as ready as I ever will be to bring the beast out into the open.

And maybe, maybe I—no, we—can start to tame it. After all.

learning to love again

Shamoli

I slept last night. After a very long time. A very, very long time. That is, for the first time since I stopped taking the sleeping pills. The doctor eased them off slowly, promising that I had not gotten addicted to them and easing them off would mean that my body got used to doing without the chemical sleep. But it didn't. At first my parents and the doctors said that it was psychological. That I should be able to sleep now, without the pills.

But they don't know my nightmares. They don't see the dark shadows looming above my bed.

Or smell the whisky on the breath.

Or feel the weight of him as he presses against me, crushing my body as his hand roughly shuts my voice.

Sometimes there are more shadows than the one. And sometimes I awake from my non-sleep to find myself in a sweat—shaking and trembling like an earthquake has hit my bed. And I need to go to the bathroom. Really, really bad. But I am too frightened to move. And besides, I'm not sure that my legs will hold me up. And so I lie there, shaking from fear and the need to go to the loo. I lie like that all night, turning towards the window to try and get the first glimpse of daybreak that would mean that I am safe again. And then turning away from the window, frightened that there is someone hiding behind the curtain, waiting to pounce. And the whole nightmare starts again.

I can't scream. For he has taken my voice from me. Not that I am a wreck without the ability to speak. Just that, when the Fear strikes, it also strikes me dumb. So my screams are trapped in my chest, choking me, along with the hands. Those hands.

Those hands weren't rough. In fact, they were creepily soft. Pudgy and soft, like there was no bone underneath. Fat, soft. But strong. Stronger than the whisky on his breath. The heat of him. The weight of him.

And I'm screaming again, deep inside my being, I'm screaming. My mouth stretched wide. My throat hurting from silent screams that scratch at me.

I have been told that it's going to get better. The psychologist has promised. But then he had promised I would sleep better. I am not blaming him, just losing faith a little, day by day. Night by night.

Finally, finally, creeping in ever so softly, little by little, sleep comes. Short naps at first. And even though I am not sleeping the whole night, my body is feeling a little rested in the morning. Finally. I am not so sure about my mind, though.

And then it's time.

I know it's useless for me to protest or resist any longer. In a way, it will be a relief to be back to school. It will give me a sense of normalcy. Or at the very least, my family will get a sense of normalcy. I don't know what normalcy feels like anymore.

As I get out of the car—my dad's dropping me. No bus for now, the car feels a bit safer. But then, but then—I have a moment of panic. Not for the first time, I wonder if everyone is going to know. Is everyone going to stare? Am I going to be branded as the 'victim'? But how would they know? No one would have told them, would they?

I feel my dad's hand on my shoulder, he is gently stroking my back. I think he is telling me, whispering to me that it's going to be all right. But it's never going to be all right. I turn towards him, to tell him that I've changed my mind. That I'm not ready. That the conversation we had two nights ago where I was feeling I could face the world again was long gone and I couldn't do it.

But then I look up into his face. His kind, kind face, the one with the twinkly eyes that no longer twinkled. Not since...since...

I dig deep into myself. If not for me, I have to do it for him. For Dad and Mum. And Nana and Nani who are suffering along with me. In a way, it must be worse for them. It was their son who had done it. It was Mum's brother who had pulled me into the darkened room when I made my way to the loo down the corridor. It was Mum's brother, it was Nana and Nani's son, it was Dad's brother-in-law with whom he'd played golf and sat on the swing outside and talked politics. It was my uncle. My Mama. It was him.

No, I have to do this. And if I back down now, I may never be able to do it again. At least not for a long, long time.

I lean over and hug Dad. At least I can do that now. For the longest time, I couldn't bear to touch or be touched. But I like that I have my father in my arms now. I am stroking his shoulder. It's me comforting him now. 'It's going to be okay, Dad. I'll be all right.' He's trying to be brave, but I can feel his shoulders tense. And then I can feel his heart beating almost out of his chest. I have to do this. For him. For them.

And then I'm standing at the gate of the school. I turn back to Dad and see him trying to be brave and confident. But his eyes are twinkly with unshed tears now. I wave at him and wave him away, a big smile on my face. Tight, tight smile. Fine, I'm going to do this. I will. I will. And I will be fine.

Abhishek

I watch as she leaves the car. The safety of the car. The safety of my arms. I can see the tremble of her shoulders and for the first time I notice how loose her clothes have become. Has she lost weight? And I haven't even noticed. I feel a stab of the guilt again. It is a handy knife that stays near my gut and wounds me all the time. I should have kept my little daughter safe. How could I have let this happen? But he was my wife's brother, of course I trusted him. Who else would I trust? No one, the knife whispers. No one...

But now she bravely steps out into the world. I know that she isn't really ready. That she's doing it for me, for her mother. And I hope, also for herself.

I watch her first tentative steps. She is literally learning to walk again. Like a little baby. She is a little girl, my little baby girl. How could he? How could he?

The tears come. I wait until she is through the gate. At least she will be safe here. Will she be safe? Shouldn't she have been safe within her own home? How could he? How. Could. He?

I drive a little way up the road, trembling and crying. I hear a car swerve and slam the brakes. I hear someone curse. Mother curses, sister curses. These are not mere words. They have horrible, horrible meanings. And we can't just throw them around like this. I look at the angry face as it drives past. 'How are you driving?' the voice shouts as the car zooms away. And I realize it was probably my fault. The driving, I mean. Not the other thing.

I can't drive anymore. I can barely see the road for my tears. I park on the side of the road and lay my head on the steering wheel. And weep. I can't drive. I can't function. I can't go home and face my wife. I hate her. I love her. I pity her.

I weep.

Mamoni

I couldn't go to school with her today. In a way, I am so ashamed of myself for not doing it. But I knew that if I went, at the moment she got out of the car, I would burst into tears. I couldn't help it. I mean, I try. I honestly do try. But I haven't been able to leave her after that. I feel so guilty, I should have been more vigilant. I should have known better. But does anyone know? Could I really have predicted that my own brother, on whose wrist I tied a rakhi all those years, the one who promised to protect me and mine was going to do this? Can anyone know such a thing? Suspect their own brother?

And if we did, what kind of world would it be? This is no longer a theoretical, rhetorical question. But a reality. A harsh, bitter, bitter reality that has swallowed my family up.

I think, amongst all of us, I was in denial the longest. How could I not be? He was the love of my life, he was my brother dammit. I feel the tears pour as soon as they drive out of the gate. I am a mess, weeping out loud, moaning and wailing. Keening as though my child has died. I thought she would. I remember seeing her. She looked as if she wasn't going to survive. How could she survive such a thing? How could I?

I had a few sessions with Shamoli's psychiatrist too. But I couldn't do what he asked me to. He wanted me to stand in front of a mirror and tell myself, 'My daughter has been raped.' And to repeat it. I tried it. Once. I said it. Once. But I couldn't after that. My brother didn't just assault one person, he assaulted her whole family. His whole family. His own family. His own niece who trusted him like he was her father.

But she is so brave. For her I will survive this. I will live and I will become strong and brave. For her. My inner lioness will have to be nurtured.

I will also have to be strong for my parents. They are wrecked as well. It was their son that did it. They are questioning themselves endlessly. Where did we go wrong? What could we have done? Is it our fault?

Is it mine?

Shamoli

I cross the courtyard towards the school building without turning back. I know that if I see Dad now, I will buckle and run back to him. So I keep my feet walking forward as my heart races backwards. Towards him. Towards home.

As I walk down the school corridor, I'm looking at the ground. I don't want to meet anyone's eye. I glance out the window and stop dead in my tracks. In the short distance, I see Dad's car. He's parked there, brake lights flashing. I try to spot him. Has something happened to his car? A flat? But no, there's no one there. Then I see some movement. Is he sitting, waiting? Is he going to wait till school's over? Is this going to be his life now? Drop me off at school and wait outside? That means I may still be in danger. Or at least that they think I may be.

Or that I am not yet clear of my depression and panic attacks. I keep watching. I wish I could get a clearer view. Oh wait, I can. I walk quickly now glancing through each window as I pass until I am almost at the end of the corridor and nearly in line with the car.

Is he asleep at the wheel? Maybe he can't sleep at night either. I know that both my parents were put onto sleeping pills too. But surely they have gone off them as well. But then I see him put his head back onto the head rest. And I see him wipe his face. I see him pull a couple of tissues from the box on the dashboard. And that's when I realize that he has been crying. Oh Dad...oh Daddy. I'm sorry, I'm so so sorry. I'd never seen my dad cry before. Mum, yes, sometimes, but him never. Dads are not meant to cry. But he's been doing a lot of it since. Since...since...he tries not to, not in front of me, at any rate, but I can see from his reddened cheeks, his watery eyes that tears have been shed. But this is the first time I've seen him cry, actually. And I am already too far away to help him. He waited till I was far enough.

I watch his shoulders shake. He is sobbing. I press my forehead against the cool window pane. I can't start crying. I can't. Not here. Not now.

Mrs Roy

Shamoli is coming back to class today. And I have to admit, I'm nervous. Shaking nervous. I over-filled my coffee cup and spilled it over the staffroom counter. Shamoli's teachers all know, of course. But not the other teachers. We're all together in a corner, like a frightened herd. None of us is sure how we're going to react, none of us has ever faced anything like this before. How much are we supposed to let on? Does she know we know? Yes, she knows some of it. We were told some of us had to know so she could come talk to us if she needed to.

I walk down the corridor and see her standing at one of the last windows. I almost want to turn and run. I shouldn't have to deal with something like this. I'm just her class teacher, not a counsellor. I'm really not ready. How can anyone be ready? Is she ready? This little child? How can she be so brave to be here? And me, wanting to turn and run like a coward. Run run, shouts my panicked heart.

But of course, I don't. I walk determinedly towards her, trying to remember the speech I had prepared. The completely inadequate and stupid speech. I didn't know anything about what she was going through—thank god—so how could I possibly say banal comments like, 'It's going to be all right?' I don't know if I can even give her a hug. I mean, wouldn't it be too strange? Besides, I have heard and read—yes, I have been doing some online research since I heard about it—that victims of sexual assault (I can't bring myself to say 'rape') hate being touched. My mind is a whirlwind of thought and then I am with her.

I open my mouth to say something. But nothing comes out. I literally don't know what to say. But I'm committed now, so I just stand by her, near her, hoping that it will be enough for now. She knows that I'm there, I can tell by the slight tilt of her head. We just stand. The bell has rung and all the students have gone into class. I can't leave her right now. So I stand. The corridor is completely quiet, and I hear her as she whispers, 'That's my Dad...' tilting her chin in the direction of a car standing outside the school.

'You want him to wait outside for you?' I guess she doesn't want to be without the safety of her parents close by.

'No, no, it's not that. I...I think...' her voice breaks, she sounds like a really small child, 'I think he's crying...'

I put my arm around her thin shoulders. I'm crying too. I lean my head closer to hers and she leans into me. And we stand there. We watch as the car slowly pulls away a few moments later. I stroke her back and she breathes in a deep, deep breath. She is girding herself to face the world alone. I wish I could be more of a help, but I don't know what else to do but be here.

Shamoli

I'm glad she's here with me. As Dad drives away, I suddenly feel very cold and vulnerable again. Alone. But she's stroking my back gently. It's when she puts her head against mine that I feel, okay, let's do this thing.

But then, I realize that the corridor is awfully quiet, that all the kids have gone into class. How am I going to go in now?

I guess there must be some panic on my face because she asks if I'd rather go to the sick room for a little while. 'Will you stay with me?' and she says she will.

We don't talk much. But I wonder what she's thinking. Is she thinking what it must have been like? I feel that's something everyone will be thinking once they see me. And I can't bear that. Because if I think it, then I want to go and wash myself again. We wait for the bell to ring and she asks me if I want to get into the class. 'It's my lesson now, so if you want, we can go in together,' she says.

I want to, I really, really want to. Now that I've seen Dad crying in the car outside, I know I've got to do this. I will do this.

'Mrs Roy, do they know? I mean, what's been said to them, why have I been away from school this long?'

'No one knows anything at all. You've been sick and in a hospital out of the city. That's all. This is information that is not ours to share with anyone. If there is someone who you'd like to talk to about it, then it is completely up to you. We are all there to help you through this horribly hard time. Any time at all, you want to talk, we are there. At least I am. Day or night. Here, here's my mobile number. Call me if you want to talk. About anything at all. The attack, or even just to chat about something if you want. Don't regard me as just your teacher now, I am very happy to be your friend, if you would like me to be that.'

I smile at her. She has obviously been preparing this speech. And she's obviously almost as nervous as I am. It's sweet. All right, I think, now I just need to take the leap of faith and face my classmates.

Mira

Shamoli walks in. She looks different, older, tired. My heart sinks into my toes. She is my best friend and I haven't had the courage to go see her. Will she ever forgive me? Can I really call myself a best friend now or even just a friend? I think I'm the only one in the class who knows what really happened, at least I hope so. I hope everyone else thinks that she was sick with something and leaves it at that. But I think I should pretend I don't know either. Because I don't know how else to react.

'Shamoli, hi,' I call out, indicating her desk next to mine. She smiles and as she comes forward, I almost hug her but stop myself in time. I just rub her arm with my hand which was already hug ready. She gives me a grin. Her lovely, open grin. And I feel the clouds begin to melt.

Yep, I have my own clouds hovering on my shoulder too. I know that someone may call me a cop out, but I know that when crisis hits, Shams is one of those who like to be left alone. She likes to know that you are there. And so I did call her a few times, asking if she wanted to come over, or wanted me to come. She said that she'd let me know as soon as she was up for it. I get that she wasn't up for it. Not for some time.

I also get that it's going to be a while before she can be comfortable with a one-on-one conversation with me. We both know there's this gigantic elephant in the room. So it's going to be easier to have a group of us around and do general chit chat. Easier for both of us. I'm cool with that for now. We'll both learn as we go along and figure it out. I really, really want to help her. I am sorry I haven't gone over to her house since. But honestly, every time I wanted to and thought of it, I lost the courage to do it. And Mum was encouraging but she didn't want to push me. Yeah, we're all out of our comfort zones here. Nothing prepares you for this.

But the only one who should be out of any comfort of any kind should be that uncle of hers. I mean, I can't imagine it. My whole faith in humanity has been impacted by what happened to Shamoli. I have my own trauma going on. I know because my psychiatrist said so. Yes, my parents decided to take me to a shrink when I started getting nightmares after finding out about what happened to my best friend. I don't know if it helped, but it certainly didn't hurt. At least I could say the kind of things, ask the kind of questions of him that I couldn't bring myself to ask my parents.

Now I think I am as ready as I will ever be. As ready as anyone could ever be. For something like this.

Shamoli

That wasn't too bad. I guess I was as ready as anyone could be. For something like this. At one point, Mira holds her hand out in a fist and I fist bump with her. And we grin. I don't know what I'm going to say later, but I can see that she knows. Like, knows knows. I hope the others don't. Mira wouldn't have told anyone else. Of that I'm sure.

Our eyes lock. She is saying sorry. Sorry for what happened to me and sorry for the fact that she didn't come. I will have to tell her that I am glad that she did not, though. I would not have been able to handle a one-on-one right away. We would not have been able to talk about anything else and I was certainly not able to talk about it.

So I try to tell her that it's okay, this is the way I wanted it. I smile back at her. It almost hurts to smile. I haven't done it in so very long. It's like my mouth has forgotten how to. I've read something about muscle memory. Not sure what it is, but it's like my mouth muscles have forgotten how to smile.

Akshat

I'm glad she's back. Though she is looking so pale. And thin. There are dark circles under her eyes that show she has not been sleeping much. And she is looking older, as though she's been away for years instead of—how long has it been? I think a month?

I smile at her. She smiles back. But it's as if she's seeing me for the first time. For a moment her face is blank. And then there is the light of recognition in her eyes. 'Hi' she mouths and I give her a thumb's up back. 'You okay?' And she nods.

I sigh. I don't know what happened to her. I know that she has been away sick with something. Not sure what it is. But my heart lurches when I see her. I want to just put my arms around her and give her a hug and tell her that I'm there for her. No matter what. But of course I can't do anything like that. We're in school. Shamoli and I were hanging around a lot. And I really liked her a lot. I mean a lot, a lot, and I think she liked me back, we never actually said anything out loud. I wanted to. I was going to. At least, I was mustering up the guts to confess to her that I really liked her. And then she fell sick and was gone. She wouldn't take my calls either. And Mira wouldn't tell me anything. I was pretty frantic. I mean, surely I should know something. I should be able to go over and see her. Unless she had something contagious. Mira promised she'd deliver my get-well-soon card to her. But I am not sure she ever did. At least, there was never any acknowledgment of it.

I thought, maybe she is not into me at all. Not that she'd be absent from school for that. She is the kind of person who would tell me that she wasn't interested. That's what I liked about her.

Now her smile reassures me. Fine, I will start from the beginning again. I am okay with that.

Shamoli

Akshat smiles. I can see that he doesn't know anything about what's happened with me. That's good. It's a relief. He and I, well, we were on the brink of something. Something really good. Something that I wanted.

But I don't know if I will ever want a relationship like that again. I mean, he's nice and everything, but I can't think of that right now. I'd love to have him as a friend. Nothing more. I can't take anything more. I know he expects more. And I don't know how I will explain to him that a friend is all he can be.

Mira

I can see that Akshat is keen to take up where they'd left off. But I don't know if Shams would be ready for a relationship like that. I'm glad he doesn't know anything. He's a very cool guy. I think he's perfect for Shams. But not now. Not yet.

'You'll learn,' I whisper to her.

She lifts her eyebrows asking what I'm talking about.

'You'll learn to love again. I promise.'

Shamoli

Mira's words have suddenly given me hope. Yes, I think, yes. Not now. Not yet. But someday, maybe, just maybe, I can learn to love again. I don't know....

Mrs Roy begins the lesson and I try to focus all my attention on what's being said.

It's actually good to be finally doing something normal for a change. And for a while, I lose myself in the present. I realize this only later. My counsellor has been telling me this is what I need. She is right. This is just what I need. I feel proud of myself that I have come to this point. There were many, many moments when I thought I could never claim this moment back again. Yet here I am.

I will claim it back again. One day at a time, one minute at a time, if that's what I need. I will do this. I promise myself.

And now I am packing my bag. My first day back is over. It wasn't as bad as I had feared it would be. In fact, it felt good to think outside the tight little box I have been inhabiting. I felt as though I was under an open sky, even in the classroom. I never loved school all that much. But I really loved being here today.

I'm a bit scared to go home now. Face everyone's questioning faces. Putting on a brave face to tell them that I was fine. But I'll put the face on. I know I can.

Anuradha

I have lain awake night after night. I haven't slept. Not at night. Not in the day. I am exhausted. But more than tired, I am so deeply hurt, so much in pain. I have been cursing myself. Where did I go wrong? How on earth did it come to this horrible pass? It must be my fault. At least a part of it. I must have given my son the feeling, the authority, that he could act in whatever way he felt like. My mind is a swarm of bees. My body moves though every bone breaks with exhaustion. My heart pains. I had to get a health check up. I am in actual pain. But the questions won't stop. The bald truth drums through me: I gave birth to a rapist, I brought up a rapist, I brought up a rapist. The words are in the air I breathe, on the path I walk. My food tastes of these words—bitter and dry. I brought up a rapist. I am the mother of a rapist. Hide your head in shame—you are the mother of a rapist. I don't know if it will ever get better. Will this voice ever calm down? Will food taste of food ever again? Will my dreams come back—will sleep?

I am in a haze of exhaustion. I see my daughter look at me with puzzled eyes. And sometimes, a few times, I have seen a spark of hate in her eyes and in my son-in-law's eyes. I see that hate and feel the revulsion. I cannot blame them. But Shamoli's eyes have never met mine after that. Not once has she been able to look directly at me. Or is it that I am not able to look at her? Has it been me all along? I know that I have not had the courage to touch her, to stroke the head that I knew was bursting with pain.

For now, I live with the ugliness. I think that I have to try and understand what happened. Why it happened.

I decide to go meet him in prison. Everyone is horrified that I have decided this. Everyone thinks that I have still not learned my lesson. But I want to explain that I am trying to learn a lesson. I am trying to find some understanding for myself. I ask Shamoli to come sit with me. I see her parents hover in the background. They are worried that I will ask their daughter to forgive my son. But that is not what I am trying to do here. I don't think I will ever forgive my son. What I am trying to do is to find a way to learn from my mistakes. Because I must have made a mistake. No well-brought-up son could turn out to become a rapist.

I put my hand on the sofa so it lies between us. I hope she will take it. But instead, she puts her own hand near mine. Is she hoping I will reach for her? We sit in silence. From the corner of my eye, I see Mamoni's hands clench into fists. But I know that she will not hit me. Not her own mother. Will she? Maybe I don't know my children well enough. I am lost in my thoughts as I feel a feathery touch against my fingers. Shamoli slides her hand closer to mine. We look at each other. Eyes lock into eyes. There is no hate in her. There is pain, there are questions, yes. But there is no hate.

I draw Shamoli close. She is finally ready to let me touch her. She couldn't at first. 'Shamoli, my darling child...' Her head is down, her hair like a shield, shutting her out. But my hand strokes her shoulder. 'Shamoli, I am not seeking your forgiveness. I am trying to understand what mistake I must have made to allow my son to do what he did to you. I am trying to understand what all of us, parents of people who go on to do this to young girls, have done wrong. I am going to try and understand, because only through that can I try and make some corrections. And maybe some changes. You understand?'

Her hair moves, her shoulders sigh. Did she just say yes?

'Shamoli, the only way I can start trying to understand is to meet him and talk to him. I am going to the prison and meeting him. Do I have your permission to do that?'

She does not move.

'I am not going to do anything without your permission. If you don't want me to go, I won't.'

We are silent. My heart slows to the rhythm of my hand stroking her shoulder. And just when I think that it is too much to expect a yes from her, I hear her.

She stirs. She sits up.

Shamoli

'Go, Nani. Go to him. I want you to look him in the eye and ask him why he did what he did. Why do any of these people do what they do? How could he do this? There are so many rapes. Every day. We need to know what goes on in the minds of these men. Yes, you are right, we need to ask him. Go, Nani. Get some answers.'

*

Last year, I wrote an article in a magazine about the need to write about sexual assault among young adults. This was in response to reports about a ten-year-old girl who was raped and became pregnant. She never told anyone and the parents did not realize until it was too late.

The letters and phone calls I got in response to the article were overwhelming. From close friends to complete strangers, so many confessed that they had been victims of such assaults in their childhood and wished that there had been a story that could have empowered them to speak up. Each and every person begged me to write such a story. So here it is.

I tried.

When writing this story, I tried very hard to find the voice of the uncle who had raped his niece. I did this because a friend in Malaysia told me that they had started a 'safe group' where rapists could talk about why they had done what they had done. The idea was to get them to talk about the shame and regret that they felt because if we isolate a criminal, he is likely to be pushed into repeating his crime. There was a lot of objection to this initiative, as many felt that once a rapist commits that crime, he loses all rights and all access to any comfort. I have to say, for the very first time, I have to agree. I think something like the crime I have just written about is so heinous, it strips the perpetrator of all rights to a sympathetic gesture.

Therefore, finding that voice of the uncle became impossible for me. The hurt is too deep. So I asked the grandmother to try and find his voice. I don't know if she did. I couldn't travel that road with her. I stood with her outside the prison, but I couldn't find it in my heart, in my words, to step in and face this man. He may be fictional, but he is real and he walks amongst us. There is a rape reported every day in the papers. And there are many that go unreported too. I knew I had to write a story about this. And so, I let the grandmother go in and face him on her own. But maybe she will come back to me and maybe she will have a better understanding than any of us has now.

If she does come and shares her story with me, I will write that story. For now, this is the best I have in me.

because superman has
better things to do

Everyone knows Superman. Even I know. Even I know, though I don't know much.

Arijit had a poster in his room. Superman flying through the air. One arm raised. He was swooping down towards a girl whose purse was being snatched. She was screaming. People were looking. But they weren't stepping forward. They were too scared. But Superman? No, he wasn't scared. He was just flying down, down, down. The robber hadn't seen him yet. And he had no idea that he was finished. He was committing his last crime.

I used to look at the poster when I was little. I used to follow my mother, room to room. I hoped that somehow, I would see Superman reach the robber and box his face. But he never did. Of course not. I know that now, but as a toddler, I kept hoping. That's what toddlers do. They hope.

Now I know better.

I liked coming to work with my mother. I loved how she could take a dirty, grimy thing and make it all shiny. As if by magic she could make old things new. I wondered where all the dirt came from. It was as if there were devils who threw dirt and slime and grime and hair in the house. But pretty soon, my mother would have it bright and new again. It was like a game. The dirt devils dirtied, my mother beat them. Again. I loved it best when she beat the carpets. Whack whack whack! The dust flew up to escape the beating, but her strong arms didn't stop. Whack whack whack!

Then, one day, Arijit was going away to boarding school and he was cleaning out his room. He took down his Superman poster and also took out lots and lots of comics. He was going to throw them away, but my mother understood the pulling at the end of her sari as I tugged and tugged without saying a word. She asked if she could take them for me. 'Maybe she can see the pictures and learn to read a little.'

And so Superman came home. I felt as if our room had suddenly become a magical place. A place where there was no danger and where I was going to be safe. Always. After all, Superman lived here now. I pored over the comics, I couldn't read them, but I looked carefully at the pictures and guessed at the story. I don't know if my story was the same as the ones the words told, but I loved my stories anyhow. And I could change them any way I wanted.

While I was alone at home, I would talk to Superman and I felt that he was talking to me. I knew he wasn't really. But sometimes, if I didn't know what to do, I would ask him and the answer would come. Because of Superman, I never felt alone. I never felt lonely or bored. I felt as if I had a best friend, even if it was just an old picture hanging on the wall. I didn't tell anyone of course. I knew that they'd make fun of me. I wasn't that stupid. I knew he wasn't real, it just felt good to have someone.

And then came the biggest change in my life. I got into school. Like big school. It was big in every sense of the word. There were so many, many people, big and small. There were huge classrooms, a huge, huge hall with a big stage where we were supposed to get together to say our prayers. There were very big toilets with big mirrors and pots behind doors. So many of them. And sinks and soap and tissues. The desks were big and the buses were bigger than any bus I had ever been on.

My uniform was big too. Too big. But it was so smart. The bigger children carried big bags but we didn't have to bring anything except a hanky pinned to our chest and a plastic tag hung from our necks. I loved my photo on my tag. I was wearing my new uniform and my hair was combed perfectly and I was smiling. Because I was happy.

Many of the other new children cried when their mothers left them at the door of the classroom. But I never cried. My mother only came with me till the bus. I would wave at her from the door, but the teacher would make me sit down next to her, so I couldn't look out of the window and see my mother. It didn't matter, I would see her in the afternoon. The teacher on the bus was very nice. She liked to talk to me. And I liked to talk to her. She always asked me what I had eaten for breakfast. And my answer was always the same—'doodh roti'.

I loved to break the hot roti up and soak it in the milk and spoon it up. Mrs Apte's breakfast was also always the same. Muesli and yogurt with a banana chopped into it. When she'd asked me if I knew what muesli was, I shook my head, too scared to even try and say the word. So next day, she brought some in a little plastic bag for me to try. It was crunchy and sweet and delicious. After she saw how much I liked it, she would bring me some every day. The other teachers were very nice too. And so were the didis who looked after us in between. Some of the children needed help to go to the bathroom. But I didn't. I could go all by myself. The boys went to one bathroom and the girls went to another. And I could tell which one was which by the picture on the door.

I liked school. I loved school. But there was one thing I didn't like. When we sat at our desks and when we had to make a circle together on the storytelling carpet, and when we had to get into the splash pool.

Many times, I sat on my own, a little away from the others. No, that is not true. I sat with them. They sat away. I didn't know why. When we were in the playground nobody pushed me on the swing. They only pushed when I tried to get into the sandbox with the others. They would push me out, not into the sandbox. I didn't know why. When we played catching-catch, no one ran after to catch me. I would run, laughing, but there was no one after me. I would stand and wait, but they would run after all the other ones who were running. Even if the den was running right past me and I was standing still, he would still not catch me.

I didn't say anything. I didn't know what to say. And to whom? Who would I tell? I knew I couldn't really explain even. And so, I started keeping away from the others. If they didn't want to be friends with me, I didn't want to be friends with them either. I sat alone during class, during playtime, during break-time. When I was all alone like this, Superman started coming to sit me. It was great. I showed him all the mean children and he promised he would help me get even with them. And he did. Like the time he opened Srijan's shoelaces with his X-ray vision and made Srijan fall down the stairs. I felt bad that he had broken his arm at first. But then, when he came back after a few days, showing off his blue plaster and he had everyone but me sign it, I didn't feel bad anymore. Superman and I just high-fived secretly, because it must have been painful, even if he was looking so proud.

Then, another time, when we had our annual play, Teacher made me Cinderella and all the children laughed and sniggered, especially when I couldn't remember all the English words. So Teacher made Gulshan take my place. I felt so bad, but I didn't tell anyone about it. Only, I told Superman. And you know what he did? On the day of the show, just as she was to go on stage, the back of her Cinderella dress ripped and she had to take Teacher's dupatta and keep it wrapped around her the whole time. She couldn't act properly because she was in tears. Yes, I know it was Superman who did that because he came and stood just behind me after that and we had a good laugh. He watched me from offstage as I sang in the chorus. I liked to sing, of course. But I would have liked it even better if I had been Cinderella and my dress would not have got torn. Because Superman was *my* friend.

It was Raghu who really started it. We were in Class 6 now. By which time I had got used to the ragging, the staying away, the holding of their noses when I passed, the fact that they would take out just one sweet when it was their birthdays and give it to me when everyone else could help themselves to however many they wanted. I also had started to understand why they did this. I didn't smell, I was as neat as they were. I was good at my studies, my books were always neat and tidy and my homework always done. I liked school, but I didn't like the other children. I didn't even notice it much anymore. And I still had Superman.

The thing that bothered me most, though, was not the bullies. They were stupid and mean, I knew that. But what about those who were not bullies? Why didn't they do anything to stop the meanness? And if not stop it, then why would they not include me in their groups, hold my hand if the teacher asked us to make a circle, or anything? Why did they just stay still and silent and watch what was happening without coming forward, or at least telling someone, like the teachers? And did the teachers not see? I would look for it and sometimes I saw the recognition in the teachers' eyes. But then they would look away, pretend it didn't happen. Or that they didn't see. Why was that? Someone should have done something. But the only one who stood up for me, and stood by me, was Superman. And I knew he wasn't really real. But he was as real as I needed him to be.

Then, I think because it wasn't bothering me anymore, or I had learnt to act as if it didn't, some of the meaner ones decided it was time to make things a little worse for me. Now it wasn't little things. It was as if the little mean things were growing up with us and becoming meaner and more serious. One day, it went out of control.

I always ate my tiffin with Superman. The others made fun of my tiffin. Nobody else brought subzi-roti to school. They brought pizzas and muffins, which were nothing but small round cakes, they brought sandwiches with chicken and something called salami. And they turned up their noses at some of the very delicious looking and yummy smelling things. Worse, instead of asking anyone else if they wanted it, they would throw it straight into the dustbin. I didn't like that. But Superman told me to hold my peace and ignore them and stay away from them as much as I could. They were not about to learn any life lessons from anyone. Least of all from me.

Superman and I began 'hanging out' as they say, at the end of the playing field where the trees were shady and the spot was lonely. The best thing was here I could talk to him out loud and he would answer me. It was the only place where we were ever alone enough to talk out loud. And soon, it became my favourite time of the day.

Then one breaktime, I was really, really sleepy. There had been no electricity at home. The whole night, the mosquitoes buzzing in my ears kept me awake. I wish they would just drink the blood they needed. Quietly. Why first wake your victim up and then take a bite? Mosquitoes are sadists, I decided. 'Sadist' is another word I had just learnt recently. When Zeenat, one of the girls in my class called Raghu a sadist for the way he kept troubling me. Not to him, just quietly to me, of course. I had to look up the word in the dictionary. I loved this new word because it described Raghu and his band of bullies so well.

Anyway, I was sleepy that day. I hadn't been able to concentrate during lessons. Without meaning to, I nodded off in my secret hiding place and was soon fast asleep.

Almost immediately, I heard the sounds of rough, sneering laughter. The sound of footsteps coming closer. At first, I thought I was dreaming.

But then, I awoke with a start, thinking that I could just run and get away. But it was already too late. I turned to Superman and asked if he was going to help. But he wasn't there. I turned to see if he was preparing himself to attack them, but he wasn't there either. He had gone. And I was alone.

'Hey, little Miss EWS, so good to know that you have learnt that your place is not with us. But we need you now.'

They surrounded me. I didn't know how many of them they were. It felt like a hundred.

'Get up, come on.' They grabbed for my tiffin and threw it on the ground. They stamped the food into the ground. I shivered. From fear, but also seeing them stepping on the remnants of my food. It was bad to put your feet on food. Everyone knew that. But they didn't care. I saw the corner of my roti turn grey with sandy dust. I looked away. Or maybe I was dragged away. I was being dragged. But I don't remember too much of it.

There was a new gymnasium being constructed. The teachers were all away in a meeting. Raghu and his pals pushed me to the construction site. There was a bowl of cement or something lying there.

'We pay your school fees, Miss EWS, you'd better put in some contribution yourself.' They had been calling me Miss EWS for some time now.

Economically Weaker Section. Poor. Yes, that was me. I was poor. Not that poor, but I didn't have the kind of home, clothes, colour pencils or cars, or any car at all, like the others had. I knew that I had got into this fancy school on the EWS quota. The government had forced schools to admit children like me. The schools probably didn't want to admit us because we took up a seat that would have gone to a paying student. But it became a law and, so, here I was. But students like Raghu didn't like it. They felt as if they were having to pay our fees. I don't know if this was true or not. In any case, it was his parents who paid his, not as if he was having a hard time himself because I was a student in his class. But he liked to make me feel inferior and like I didn't belong. And I didn't. Not really. But there was a law and why should I not take advantage of that and study where they studied? It would be one thing if I was wasting the chance by not studying. But I was working really hard, concentrating really well and going for after school tuition for English and Maths like I was supposed to. I was working much harder than Raghu was, I'm sure of that. Yet, he felt he had more of a right to be here than I did.

And now I was standing in the construction site. Anshu was trying to lift a platter of cement.

'Ughhh! It's dirty,' he squealed. Raghu's grin became even wider. He loved seeing anyone at all in any kind of problem. Even if he was a friend.

Raghu pulled at my arm. His fingers, hurting, dug into my skin.

'Right, Miss EWS, it's payback time. Got it? We pay school fees for a labourer, you need to put in some labour yourself.' He pushed me towards the bowl of wet cement. I didn't know what he wanted me to do. I knew it was going to be something horrible, but I didn't know what. So I just stood there.

'Try not to look as dumb as you are. At least try and put some intelligence into your stupid face.'

I still didn't know what he wanted. I would do it if I knew. Anything to finish this. Anything to let him get his fun out of it and then be on his way. His gang sniggered. I could see Manu was trying to laugh, but he wasn't really finding this very funny. Good, there was some good in at least one of them.

I stared at Manu. If I could make contact with him, maybe he would stand up for me. But he was looking studiously away as though there was something hugely interesting in the bushes that shielded us from view. I wished Superman was real, that he would somehow show up and flatten Raghu and his gang to the floor.

'Pick it up,' Raghu commanded, pointing at the bowl of cement. Okay, I thought, fine, I'll just do what he wants and get over with it. I bent over the bowl, I tried to pick it up. I didn't mind the dirt. But as I lifted, I realized that the bowl was much, much heavier than it looked. I tried again, but I couldn't even lift it one inch off the ground. I wished I could, I wished I had Superman with me. I would have lifted it with his help and dumped the whole bowl onto Raghu's stupid head. I would have the last laugh.

But obviously, Superman had better things to do than hang out and help a poor girl. Superman was off saving lives and this was just a tiny blip on his radar. Look, I am not that stupid, I knew that there wasn't really a Superman, I knew that he was just a comic book and sometimes a movie character, though I'd never seen his movies. I knew that. But somewhere, thinking that I had him by my side gave me courage. Gave me a buddy who would be there when I needed him. I needed him right now. I needed him more than I had ever needed anyone. Or anything. But he was off, being a comic book hero. And I was on my own. I had to be my own Superman. Or Superwoman. Or just be brave. Really.

I stood up, looked Raghu in the eye. I tried to stop my voice from shaking, 'If I am to lift this, you or someone is going to have to help me. It's very heavy.'

'Very heavy or are you too weak? Why don't you admit that you are just a poor little chick pretending to be rich? Face it, you are never going to be one of us.'

And that's when I broke. I couldn't stand his sneering voice. 'I don't want to be one of you. Nobody wants to be one of you. No one in their right mind. Who would want to be a bully and a mean, mean boy?'

I sounded stupid. And weak. But when I get angry, I can't think of any English. And if I spoke in Hindi, then it would make them laugh at me even more. Which was stupid. I had heard them trying to speak Hindi and it was really something worth laughing at. Fine, they spoke better English. But I spoke better Hindi. But somehow, one was okay and the other was to be made fun of. But I was not in a position to say any of this. These people did not know any logic. And there was no sense at all in what they thought or did or anything.

'No one wants to be *me*?' his voice was harsh, but I think he was also shocked. Shocked that I had answered back at all.

'No one in their right minds...' the words seemed to be coming out of somewhere totally different. Like, these were not my words. I could never ever speak like this. But I was loving this new version of me, so I pushed on.

'See these jokers of yours, your pet puppies. They want to be you. But they may not ever be able to be you. I don't think that any of them is mean enough, nasty enough to be the true you. They are stupid enough, but not mean enough, you know.'

'Wow, thanks for the psychobabble, you...you Dalit...' he spat. 'Yeah, I know you're a stupid backward schedule caste who is trying to hang out with us, but you are just poor and dirty.' He moved a step or two closer. I could see he had expected I would back down. But I stood my ground. I looked over at Manu, glanced, really. He was uncomfortable with the ugly turn this had taken. I knew if I brought some attention to him, then the bullies were likely to leave me alone and turn on him. But there was something like...admiration in his eye when he caught my glance. No, I wasn't going to give him up for the feeding frenzy I knew was headed my way. A pack of cowardly hyenas these were. I had watched a programme on Africa and the hyena pack had really reminded me of Raghu and his toli of followers.

'Tujhe pata hai ki agar maine complaint kee, you could be thrown out of school for calling me a Dalit? Don't you read the newspaper? Oh wait, tujhe toh padna hee nahin aata, na?'

I decided right there and then that I was not going to let him or anyone else make me feel ashamed of talking in Hindi. If I could say it better in Hindi, I would say it in Hindi.

'Huh, it's you who's going to get thrown out of school, stupid, not me. Do you even know the meaning of psychobabble?' Before anyone could move, he stuck his hands into the wet cement and picked up two gobs of the stuff and flung it at me. It flew at my face, my hair, my precious, clean uniform. I wiped it off my forehead but some of it was already in my eyes. And it hurt. If I ever needed Superman, I needed him now. But I was on my own. As I tried to get the cement out of my burning eyes, I noticed that some of the cement had also flown on to Raghu and a couple of his friends. I felt a bubble of laughter rise within me.

'Let me tell you a little saying you have probably never heard before. Jab keechar kisi ke upar pheko, kuch keechar tumhare upar bhi chipakti hai. You've done as much harm to yourself as you think you've done to me. You, Raghu, are a kaayar.'

He looked at me blankly.

'Do you even know the meaning of kaayar? Probably not. It means coward, that's what you are. A coward with no...' and then I couldn't think of what to say. I searched around. I looked up and Manu was standing right behind Raghu. Manu mouthed the word 'guts'.

'GUTS. A kaayar is a person who has no guts. See, I know the word kayaar, but you don't know the word coward...' I realized that I'd just said that the wrong way around. But he was so shocked, he didn't even notice, so I stopped myself from correcting the sentence.

I could see his rage building and knew I had to distract him somehow. 'Can I help you wipe the cement off?' I stepped up to him so that we were almost nose to nose.

'Don't touch me,' he almost yelped. He looked

down and saw the cement on his shirt and wiped it with his hands, quite forgetting that his hands were full of cement. As the grey mess spread further, I felt a bubble of laughter grow within me. I burst out laughing, pointing at him.

This was probably a mistake, an already enraged Raghav flew at me. Instinctively, I ducked and stepped aside.

My eyes blurred with tears and I was so shocked, I couldn't move. But then, Raghu was going backwards. He was standing, and now he was falling right next to me. I couldn't understand what was happening. I turned my head and momentarily Raghu and I were looking each other eye to eye. I stared, why was he lying down next to me? Then I felt someone pull me up. My face hurt, my head hurt. I touched my head and my hand came away bloodied. I looked up from my hand to find Manu standing there. He had his arm on my shoulder. 'It's okay, you're okay. Are you? Are you okay?'

I nodded, yes, I was okay, I think.

I looked down at Raghu. How did he get to the ground?. Had I hit him? No, I don't think so. He made as if to get up.

'Don't move, don't you dare move,' said Manu,

putting his foot on Raghu's chest to stop him getting up. 'You move a muscle and I'll hit you.'

It was Manu. Manu had knocked Raghu down. Amazing. I looked around. None of Raghu's hangers on were to be seen. They had run like frightened kaayars the minute all this began.

Raghu groaned and still lying there on the ground, he spat at Manu, 'I always knew you were a good-for-nothing useless Dalit lover. Idiot. I never liked you. Get out of my sight. I never want to see you two again. Go back to where you belong in your untouchable slum.'

Manu leaned forward to take another swing at Raghu. But I didn't want to be saved by someone else. I was a girl who did not need a boy to defend her. I mean, why should I? There was no Superman, and I didn't need anyone to be him for me.

'Wait,' I put my hand on Manu's raised arm. 'Wait, let me handle it.'

'Listen, you cement-handed clumsy bully. This is the very last time you are going to use curse words on me. Yes, I am a Dalit and I am a girl and I am a student here in this school. But guess what, you are none of those things. This is the last time you are going to see either of us. Because you've just had your last day at this school. You are going to get thrown right out of here so fast, you won't even see it happening.'

'Bye bye, enjoy your life. We are sure going to enjoy school much more now that you're not in it.' Manu turned me by my arm and we started heading towards the principal's office. This time, Raghu had gone way way too far.

'You're going to get into trouble, you shouldn't have hit him,' I said to Manu, though of course I was pleased.

'Huh? Me? No, I didn't hit him. It was you. You suddenly went bat crazy and hit him. Wait, you don't remember?'

I was laughing. I don't know when I had hit him. But yes, my knuckles hurt and were red. 'I hit him...' I wasn't asking, I was realizing. 'Am I in trouble? Am I going to get thrown out of school along with that...that....' I was struggling to find the right words.

'Kaayar,' said Manu helpfully. We were giggling.

Suddenly there was a cry from behind us. 'Guys, guys...wait...wait.'

We turned. Raghu was struggling to get up off the ground. His hands were stuck. The cement had hardened and set his hands onto the grass.

Manu and I looked at Raghu. He looked so pathetic, calling out to us to help him. We burst into the longest, loudest laughter that I have ever laughed in my whole life.

walk the straight line

By the time they laid me by the side of the court, I had already exited my body.

I floated above myself as they rushed nurses and water and phone calls and faces around me. I wished they'd stop. I wished they would just let it go. Let me go. I wished. It to. Stop. Dead.

By the time they laid me by the side of the court. I had already exited my body.

Lights. Camera. Action. No, wait, not action. No action. I can't move. Nothing moves. I am tied into submission. The lights are too bright. The beeps too loud. I close my eyes, but my lids don't shut the lights out. I try to put my hands to my ears. But nothing moves. I try to breathe. But my nostrils don't pull in air and my lungs won't inflate. I am drowning. Am I drowning? I am suffocating. I struggle. At least I think I struggle. But I'm not sure if anything moves.

Dark. All is dark. I float away.

Lights. Camera. Action. Wait...action? I think I move. A finger moves. I think. Does it? I breathe in. The cold air hurts my nostrils and my lungs don't like it.

Dark. Lights. Silence. Noise. Too loud. Complete silence.

It goes on like that. I don't know how long. Until, like water drops in an ocean comes the realizsation that I am still alive. Not much. But some. I have lost all sense of time. All sense of...everything really.

Then come the words. One by one. Again, like a tiny drop in a deep, deep ocean. A dark ocean, I begin to hear words. Drop by drop. My name, my name. Over and over. And I want to answer. I do. But nothing moves. If only I could see.

I can see. Blurry. Shapes. Broken. Images. The light hurts. It's too bright. Shut out the lights. I scream. The faces hover overhead. But the lights don't dim. Do I see them really? Or do I just sense the faces? And recognize them from memory?

I can hear breathing. Deep, slow breaths. Someone is asleep. Near me. Someone moves. Rustling sheets. Someone breathes. Near me. If only I could turn.

Slowly, painfully slowly. It all comes back. But not when they are near me. There is a man I don't know. White beard and kind eyes. Is he God? This is what God should look like. If God was a man. If there is a God. I smile. The face comes closer. God floats above me. Smiling back.

'Welcome,' he says in a voice that is pleasantly gravelly. And that's when I realize that my senses are back. More than back. Heightened. Sharp. The smell of disinfectant, the clarity of his eyes. The sharply etched fine laugh lines around his mouth and eyes. Surely there should be music when you're entering heaven. Is this heaven?

Am I dead?

'Am I dead?'

'Are you God, then?'

His laugh is nice. Low and deep.

Turns out, I'm not dead. And he's not God.

He is a sort of head doctor. Not a shrink. Although he tells me there will be a shrink soon. And in answer to my why, come tears. Mine.

And then there are more tears. Other's. Mothers' (I actually do have two), my dad (just the one) and little brother. Everyone is crying. They are pleased to have me back. I was gone, almost dead for days. But I am back now.

I am back and I have to face that it was my fault. It was my doing. I shouldn't have done it. And I was clever enough to hide it. Oh, I was practically hiding it from myself, even. For who would willingly be doing what I was doing, hate it, loathe it and continue to do it. The first sign of insanity is doing the same thing over and over and expecting different results. And that was what I was up to. Even though I kept telling myself that I should stop, the high always made up for the low. No matter how low that low was.

It was just a tiny first step. So easy. Everyone was doing it. And there seemed no downside then. Yeah, not everyone, but so many. We just tried it for the first time on a lark. At a party. It was a really small pill and a bit of beer and it felt so incredible.

Okay, long story short. I became a drug addict.

I was taking just party pills at first. Tiny pills that didn't taste of much. It was easy to smuggle them anywhere. No one else needed to know. No one did.

Then it became lines of cocaine. And then it came to a place where anything at all would do. Glue, markers, oh anything and everything so that I was flying high almost all the time.

No one knew. I was doing okay in studies. Sometimes the drugs would help me concentrate on what I was studying. Sometimes it paid off when I could fly through the exam paper on the wings of drug-induced knowledge. Though a couple of times the crash came just as the paper was handed out and I'd be left a sweaty mess of empty brain and nothing to show for all those sleepless nights.

Some of my friends tried to stop me when they got to know. I promised them that I would. Swore I was done with it. And they believed me. Why shouldn't they? I was fine. Even when I was high, they couldn't always tell. I wasn't hanging around with them too much now, keeping more to myself. My parents tried to find out what was up with me, but they put it down to teenage angst. I could glibly lie to them if they asked. Now I don't remember what I'd told them.

A friend even threatened to tell my folks about it, but I swore that I was done with it and we shouldn't hassle them especially after all that they had been through. My parents had been through a pretty painful divorce and my mother had the added pain and humiliation of seeing my father get married soon after. So it wasn't hard to tell my pal that there was no need to bother them anymore. It would be easy to tell myself and others that it was my parents' breakup that had pushed me over the edge and caused me to find shelter in drugs.

But that was not the truth. I could admit that to myself. In fact, it all began when everything was just cool and fine at home. My parents were kind of distant from each other, each involved in their own lives and work and looking after their respective parents. To anyone looking from the outside, all was fine in the Kalra household.

But sometimes smooth surfaces don't show what's really going on. My father was seeing someone from his office. So clichéd, really. And my mother was busy at work after she'd got a big promotion. She was happy. She loved her job in a big multinational company. Yes, it all sounds as though I've copy pasted this from a cheap potboiler, but I guess things become clichés because they are true. At least some of the time. Like in this case.

I was in my school basketball team. It helped keep me in shape and those were the times that I felt more alive than at any other. I am not going to blame anything—not my actions, not my habits on anyone else. At least there's that. I do take responsibility. Wholly and solely.

I loved basketball, I didn't detest school. I had some friends. I just tried that one little pill which then took over my life. I had never thought it would. I had, in fact, sneered at some others I knew who allowed things to become their masters. I felt I could be the master of my own destiny. And I hated the thought of anyone or anything dictating what I did or how I did it.

But a little white pill did. It became my master. And my mistress, because I so fell in love with it that she completely blinded me to real girls out there. She seduced me to try the others that came along with her—cocaine, booze, you name it. When I was already far gone, I was willing to try anything else that would carry me higher.

There were days when I couldn't show up for basketball practice. But I was good and I was in the team, so I didn't get thrown out, although I did get the occasional earful from the coach. Water off a duck's back, really, as his words would roll off my drug-induced armour.

Yup, that is what I felt. I was wearing an armour and nothing could penetrate or hurt me. I knew to keep my mouth shut and I was good at conjuring up a contrite face. So no one was the wiser and I certainly was not wiser either.

There were also times when I wasn't on anything. Either because I couldn't get my hands on anything or because I had promised myself, for the hundredth time, that it was time to quit. At those times, I felt totally exposed and naked. It was like I was stripped down to the skin and bone and anybody and everybody could do what they wanted to me. At those times it was worse, I was more paranoid and suspicious of everyone, more like a freak than when I was actually high.

It was at these times that my parents would worry and wonder if there was something wrong. As soon as I saw that look on their faces, I knew that I would have to fix it by getting a fix myself. I would literally move heaven and earth until I found what I was needed. Then all would be right with the world again. Once again, I was within my protective shell and I felt back on balance, my parents thinking they had resolved my teenage angst.

When I was off, I couldn't walk a straight line. I'd weave like a drunk. And when I was on, I could walk straighter, shoot more accurately, write better, study sharper. In short. Bliss.

I think I was in that state of in-between that day—half high, half low. We were in the middle of a game. I was running through a haze. I wasn't high enough and I was struggling. I had tried to get my hands on some fresh stuff, but hadn't had the time. And so, although my stocks were running a bit low, I thought I could wait till after the game. Turned out I couldn't.

As the game progressed I felt the world kind of thicken and blur. Someone threw the ball at me. Someone else came at me from another direction. My mind's wires got crossed. I ran straight into the person as the ball hit my head. I kept going till I went down. Hard.

And then sky. Ground was replaced with sky. I hit my head on the court. At least that's what they tell me now. I wasn't aware enough to know. I was rushed to hospital and I was in a coma of sorts. I don't know, they tell me technical terms that turn to cotton wool inside my head. And I don't really care anyway.

Am I glad that I am alive? Am I? I honestly can't answer that question. I know one thing though. I wish I could persuade someone to get me some stuff. I desperately need it. I am a wreck without it. The painkillers help some. But I am way beyond that. They're too mild really. I wish my friends would visit. The ones who can sneak some in for me. But I am on limited visitation. Close family only. And they are not about to oblige.

I cry and my parents think that it's from the pain. Or from the fact that I almost died. Or that I've lost time. They don't know how much time I have really lost. There are huge gaping holes in my life like a bullet-ridden wall. They are happy that I am alive. Of course they are. But would they be if they knew all that I had been up to? Or would they think that it would be better if my head had smashed a little bit harder and I had gone into the big sleep once and for all—not this silly out for a few days, then back to being a half-wit. And maybe more than the half-wit that I was.

It strikes me then, almost as hard as my head on

concrete. Have I regained all my faculties? Or am I going to be damaged goods from now on? Am I going to be in a wheelchair for the rest of my life? I sweat and cry with fear. Surely not. Surely not. I have to find out. I ask to see the doctors.

My parents hover and luckily the doctor asks to talk to me on my own. I am glad. I want to be able to ask all that I need to ask.

But it seems I must wait. The doctor wants to say all that he needs to say first.

And what he wants to say is that he knows I am an addict. My parents know too.

Wait. Really? And they haven't ranted and raved and shouted and fussed about it? I am in shock all over again. I mean, if it had been me, I would have beaten me to within an inch of my life. Or at least a few tight slaps. But all they've done is be there. Quietly, lovingly. Hmm....

The doctor asks me why and I don't know what to say. I mean, is there really an answer?

Fine. I'll come clean.

Finally, finally, some guilt is kicking in. I have been waiting for guilt for a while. But she was elusive. Now, she is here to stay. Guilt is supposed to be a negative thing but right now she is making me take a few steps in the right direction. I'll take them. Gradually the shaking is wearing off, the cold sweats, the wretched cold turkey blues. I can feel myself healing. I don't always like it. I don't always appreciate feeling this whole again. I prefer the holes to the whole. But at least I can be clever with words again. And I know, I don't want to go back there again. I hope I can stay the course. It's a long road back. But I can try.

going off grid

That's it. I've had enough. Not interested anymore. I don't care.

I can't.

I can't care.

Care.

It doesn't help anyway.

Not even a drop of difference.

So what's the point? Of caring, of raging, of arguing, fighting, crying? What's the point?

Yes, there was a time when I cared. There was a time till this evening that I did care. And raged and argued and fought and yes, cried. Buckets.

But I am done. I can't do this anymore. It takes a great big toll on me personally, and it makes no difference anyway. So what's the point?

My phone buzzes and flashes blue. Compulsively, I pick it up.

Anan: u ok?

Me: ya

Anan: u sure?

Me:

Anan: u still there?

Me: ya

Anan: u not ok r u?

Me: :\

Anan: wanna talk?

Me: no, not right now…I can't

And I actually can't. My parents have imposed a no-phones-after-ten-on-school-nights rule. Which is stupid. Who does that? I don't. I am on the phone, but with the ringer off and under my bedclothes because I don't want the glow of the phone to give me away through the crack under the door. But I can't talk, my voice would carry.

Besides, I don't really want to talk. Not right now. I'll talk later, of course I'll talk with Anan, but right now I need to talk with myself. I have a lot I need to say. But to myself.

No. Correction. I have nothing to say, not much. Just a decision. And I have made that decision. That I am done. I can't fight these battles anymore.

I know Ma and Papa will be disappointed. They have brought me up to care. To fight and to speak up for the voiceless. To fight back against injustice. But what's the point? Nothing changes. My voice falls on deaf ears, my appeals on cold hearts.

So here is my decision. I am not going to care. I am not going to look or hear or act. No matter what. And yesterday helped me come to that decision.

Yesterday. A turning point in my life. I really lost the battle that I was struggling in vain to fight. Like I always do. There was a puppy on the street and these boys were running after it, throwing stones and laughing gleefully. Not only that, they had tied a couple of old tins to his little legs so that when he ran, the cans rattled and banged and sometimes hit his hind legs as he tried to escape. I saw red. My voice takes on this horrible shriek when I get mad angry. I couldn't bear to see them behave like this, to see how much these stupid boys were enjoying this. I am constantly amazed when people enjoy cruelty. Like, I just don't get it. I am not a goody-two-shoes like some of my classmates claim I am.

But how can you choose cruelty? Don't be kind, don't be mushy, okay. But why be cruel? How can you get a kick out of seeing someone or something suffer, let alone making them suffer? It makes my blood run cold and makes it boil all at the same time. Not a comfortable thing to be.

And by the way, when people say, 'He behaved like an animal' when someone is doing something horrible, I fight that as well with a, 'It's only humans who would do that, animals never behave like this. And if by chance they ever did, we would have to say that it behaved like a human.'

Anyway, this isn't about animal rights. Well, it's not only about animal rights. It about rights. Period. Everyone's rights. Yours as much as mine as much as anyone else's—human or animal. Yeah, I know I am sounding quite like that goody-two-shoes I was denying being just now, but I can't believe that someone would think that just speaking up against injustice should be thought of like that. It is not. It is just common sense, nothing more. And nothing less.

Okay, I don't want to ramble. I know that I am in an emotional, confused state. I know that I have got to face the facts.

Yesterday, I really, really lost it. Like lost it to

the extent that I almost lost my voice. That's how mad angry I was. I shouted and the boys just turned their attention to me, laughing, pointing.

From the corner of my eye I saw that the puppy had sought refuge under a car and lay cowering there. But they would find him easily. And not just because one of the tin cans on a string was trailing out from under the car. They would continue to torture the pup again. As long as no one stopped them, they would do so. If not with this pup right now, then another somewhere else. They would torture those who could not fight back as long as there was no one fighting for them.

So 'tag, you're it' and there I was screaming at the top of my lungs, as I often do.

People stopped and stared. People looked uncomfortable. People started to snigger. And then to laugh. The laughing became a roar. The boys who had stopped to gape began to laugh as well and pretty soon, all eyes were on me. All fingers pointed at me and I was an object of ridicule.

My face was red, but no longer from my red hot anger. I was burning with embarrassment. I was so ashamed. I didn't know exactly how to back down. I stood there, shaking. Not one person. Not one came up to take my side. Each and every person there thought I was being stupid for trying to help a helpless puppy from being tortured. No one thought they should help me. Or the pup. Standing there, I wasn't so sure myself. It was just one more puppy among the thousands who get hit and run over or starved or tortured. Even if I helped this one for a little while, what difference was I going to make? None. If I stopped one boy from teasing one girl, one student from bullying another—so what? It was one in a billion. It was barely even a single drop in a whole wide ocean. So why bother?

I was lost in this realization when it swept over me that I was the one who was stupid and misguided. I was the one who was fighting a battle that was lost before it began. There was always going to be only one of me and many of the others. Surely it would be just easier to simply drop all these so-called causes I took up in an endlessly predictable drumbeat and just learnt to mind my own business. After all, my life was good. Everything was fine. Nothing of anything I did was ever going to change the world, so why not just be happy and grateful for all I had and learn to blinker out anything that made me uncomfortable.

Sorry, puppy.

I moved. I couldn't stand it any longer. The boys hesitated, wondering if I was leaving or coming for them. I was leaving. I walked past the puppy. I heard him whimper. My heart broke, but my feet kept moving on guided by my oh-so-sensible brain. 'There's nothing you can do there's nothing you can do there's nothing you can do' clacked the train of my thoughts. My eyes didn't see where I was going, they'd gone too blurry. My heart was heavy with guilt for having left that poor puppy there. But I couldn't do anything. We already had three rescued dogs, we really couldn't afford another and sending it to some shelter was like putting it out of my mind, out of the range of my guilt. That's all. Who knew what it would have to survive there. It was a street dog and no one adopts those.

But how could I explain that I had taken a decision to stop trying to change the world. How could I tell my mother, my father that all that they had taught me was going to be of no use. That I was done. So instead, I wept. Buried my shoulder into Papa's chest and wept.

I think I said, 'I can't do this anymore,' out loud, but I am not sure if I only just thought it.

So, after some coaxing from both my parents and a hot chocolate sundae, I told them what had happened. I wept when I came to the part of me leaving the whimpering puppy and wondering whether the boys dragged him out again. I felt terrible. But I could not shake the humiliation of the people around laughing and pointing. It was me over the puppy. And I chose me.

'And did it feel alright? Like you had done the right thing?'

I thought about it. 'No,' my voice was small. I'd known the answer to this already. Of course I didn't feel good about it.

'But what choice did I have? They were all laughing.'

'Did their laughter hurt you?'

'Yes,' I was defiant, 'yes, their laughter was humiliating.'

'Did it hurt you more than the pup was being hurt?'

'But what could I do...?' I wailed. 'I couldn't bring him here. And there are so many pups out there and even more horrible people doing horrible things to anyone and everyone they can. I can't change the world. I'm just a kid. You guys don't seem to remember that. This is too much responsibility.'

It's true. They expected too much from me. My friends' parents didn't expect so much. They told my friends to stay out of harm's way, be safe. Leave trouble alone. My parents on the other hand, seemed to be urging me to head towards trouble and sort it out. But I was still a child, they seemed to forget that.

'If you haven't been able to change the world as adults, why do you expect me to?'

'No, you're right, maybe we made a mistake in encouraging you to step forward when you see something or someone being harassed. Maybe it is better to look the other way, turn a deaf ear to those cries of help. After all, everything is not your business. It is what most people do, so why not you too?'

Wait, what? They were agreeing with me? It was going to be okay for me to walk away, go off the grid? Is that what they were really saying. Or were they trying some reverse psychology stuff on me? I narrowed my eyes suspiciously at them.

'So it's okay that I left the pup?'

'Well, your Ma and I would not have left him.

But you are old enough now and it is perfectly fine for you to take your own decisions on these matters. After all, why should you have to do everything that we do?'

'So you wouldn't have walked away?' I challenged them. It was a me versus them right now. They shook their heads.

'And what about the sneering, jeering public?'

'What about them?'

'It was horrible, okay? Everyone was laughing at me. Not one of them was willing to come to the dog's rescue or to mine.'

'Of course it was horrible. If it were easy, everyone would do it. Everyone would be Gandhiji. But it falls upon a chosen few to step forward. Maybe no one came to your rescue. But so what. You came to someone else's rescue. You were strong enough to take up that challenge. Why would you need to be rescued yourself?'

'I could never be Gandhiji.'

'Maybe not. But to the person you helped, you would be Gandhi.'

I noticed Papa rummaging through the newspapers stacked behind the dining table. He came back reading out loud from an article. It was about someone who did an analysis and found that we were a nation of apathetic bystanders. That is why so many bad things happened. Public attacks and such, because the perpetrators always thought, or rather knew that no one was going to step forward to help the victim.

'Now,' he said, folding the paper, 'suppose there is suddenly one person who does use her voice. One person who speaks up and acts and makes an attempt to stop it. Bystanders may be surprised, but some may even admire the girl's courage and think, "I could do that, I should do that." Next time something happens in front of them, they may be the one to step forward, remembering how you had done it. They may even be the one being laughed at. But there may be someone in *that* crowd who thinks "I could do that." And then you have started a movement. A journey really does start with just one step. So why be scared to taking that first step?

'There are things—wrong things—that for a long time were considered all right, acceptable, even. But now we know better because there was that one person who stood up and objected.'

'Like what?'

'Well, this morning's paper has an article about

a powerful businessman who used to inappropriately touch women and it was supposed to be taken as a joke. Now, because someone stood up and said "no", others too took strength from that and added their objections and the man has apologized. It is not going to be that easy for anyone else to do it now.'

Ma put her arm around my shoulders and said, 'And maybe one day, the circle will complete itself. Maybe someday you will need someone to step up for you. We would like to know there will be others who will help at that time, wouldn't we?'

I thought back on things. Little things. This girl in our school who had stood up for a boy when people teased him about the pee bag he had to carry. That woman who had forcibly taken away a dog from his owner because he was being mistreated and tied up all the time. The bigger things like the Chipko Andolan where people would hug trees to prevent them from being cut down. The Bell Bajao Andolan where neighbours were ringing doorbells if they heard sounds of domestic violence coming from someone's house.

There's a girl who has become a well-known writer after she began a blog that gave space to women who had suffered physical and sexual abuse.

She even got a group of lawyers to join in and give free advice to women who could post anonymously if they wanted or needed to. Apparently, some lawyers had taken on cases through the blog and won them in court. They got paid only after the settlement was made. It was something called *pro bono*.

I'm sure there were people who laughed at those who started off with these objections. It must not have been easy. But it brought about change.

I sighed. 'Okay, okay, I get your point. I'll get back on the grid. I'll rescue that puppy, or whatever.'

'Why don't we all go out and search for him? Maybe we can find a home for him? Should we go look for him?'

And we were off. I was back on the grid.

acknowledgements

Writing is known as a solitary activity. But in my case, it takes a village to write a book. So I want to thank my village.

Thanks to my mother, whose fortitude and companionship through her illness, her pushing me to write this book despite the odds we were facing gave me the strength to shelter in stories. This book has been a long, internal journey of discovery.

To the many, many children who I meet through my work, who trust me with their stories and experiences. I would be stranded without you. Thanks to all the schools who, in one way or another, get their students to read my work, especially those schools that prescribe my books for classroom discussions and invite me to interact with the students. I am so grateful that you connect me with my readers.

Mita Kapur and Siyahi, my agent, who had the confidence in me to sign on a two-book deal. It terrified me and froze me, but I was warmed by your faith in me.

Ravi Singh, years ago you came all the way to my home to tell me that you wanted a book from me because you had loved *Weed* which had just come out. It gave me confidence in my words. So finally, here is my gift to you and your gift to me.

My publisher, Speaking Tiger, thank you for your patience. Sorry this took so long.

And then, my family, all of them whose companionship is a warm blanket on a cold night, and cool shade when the sun is too hot—in short, all that I need.

My children whose flights to success are my own wings.

To Keshav, as always, who roots me and nourishes my soul.